LA JORNADA

Jeb Logan was a Southerner in the Arizona territory. His father, Colonel Wentworth Logan, had been murdered and the vengeance trail led into some of the roughest, meanest country in the West. Jeb was a kid—too young, some folks said. But he knew what he had to do. Nothing could stop him once he started—not Apache raids, a brutal bull-whipping in public, or a duel with death and dishonor staring him straight in the face.

LA JORNADA

Walt Coburn

GUNSMOKE

This hardback edition 2006
by BBC Audiobooks Ltd
by arrangement with
Golden West Literary Agency

ISBN 1 4056 8061 X

British Library Cataloguing in Publication Data available.

Printed and bound in Great Britain by
Antony Rowe Ltd., Chippenham, Wiltshire

1

THE TWO men rode into the raw black wind that whipped the dry snow from the ragged peaks of the Rincons and carried it down across the mesquite and cholla desert, where it was lost in the desert sand.

One of the riders was a tall white man, with a stubble of dark whiskers under a dusty black handkerchief pulled up across his mouth and aquiline nose. Above this protective mask his red-lidded eyes squinted ahead into the night.

The other rider was a giant Negro on a blue army mule. Darkness hid the hard, etched lines of suffering and the bluish-grey pallor of his face.

"How're you doing, Bugler?" The white man's voice sounded harsh from the cold and long silence.

"Makin' out, Cap'n Jeb." The mellow voice was strained.

The white man reined his horse in the lee of a cutbank. "This is as good a place as any to lay over till daybreak," he said, dismounting. "Easy does it, Bugler." Jeb lifted the wounded Negro gently from the saddle to the ground.

The wind whipped the sand into their faces as he pillowed the Negro's head on a rolled saddle blanket. He unscrewed the top from a canteen and helped the wounded man hold it steady.

"How much water's left, Cap'n Jeb?"

"Plenty," lied the white man. "Drink all you need."

Jeb unsaddled and tied his horse and the mule on picket ropes. He kindled a small fire and eased the wounded man near the warmth of the wind-whipped blaze.

"Supposin' 'em 'paches sneak up, Cap'n Jeb?"

"Not likely," Jeb answered. "From the map I calculate we're within a few miles of Tucson. This dry wash should empty into the Santa Cruz River."

"Supposin' you leave me here to rest; scout on ahead

5

till you locate Tucson. Then come back and fotch me in. Me'n 'at ol' blue mule."

"We're doin' all right." Jeb took a pint flask from his pocket and uncorked it. "See what this'll do for you." He held the flask against the blue lips until the wounded man swallowed a couple of times.

"Mebby there ain't much time left, Cap'n Jeb. You plumb sho' you got the description of 'at man? You got it fixed in yo' mind?"

"I'll know him when I meet him, Bugler."

"You got 'at map showin' where I buried the Colonel?"

"I got it on paper, Bugler. And inside me."

A strong gust of wind swept the sand over them. When the Negro began coughing, the white man held him while he hemorrhaged a crimson flow on the dry sand. Gently he wiped the flecks of blood from the sick man's mouth with a soiled handkerchief. Dark eyes rolled back in the ashen face and his words were whispered and incoherent. Jeb brought a battered old brass bugle from one of the saddle pockets and the black hands closed caressingly over it. A smile crossed the blue lips.

Bugler died there like that.

Jeb covered him with a saddle blanket. The canteen and the whisky flask were both empty.

The white man held his numbed hands close to the blaze for warmth. Then he kicked sand over the fire, blotting it out, and sat hunched over, his back to the raw wind. His two Colt guns ready in their holsters, the two picket ropes within reach, he kept his lonely vigil beside his dead companion until the first streak of dawn filtered through the dust haze.

Weary and empty-bellied, his tongue thick as flannel, he sat with memories crowding his brooding thoughts. Bugler, the old Negro, had worshipped Colonel Wentworth Logan of the Confederate Army, and had travelled with him into Mexico. With the end of the Mexican War, they went together into the mountain and desert wasteland of Pimeria Alta, known, after the Gadsden Purchase, as Arizona Territory.

And now Jeb Logan, charged with an extraordinary mission, was alone, a stranger in a strange country. He had come into Arizona Territory to kill the man who had murdered his father, whom he had loved and respected above all men on earth.

Colonel Wentworth Logan, who had been a Judge of the Supreme Court, was a polished gentleman by breeding and education. He was diplomatic, and possessed a keen legal mind. He spoke the Mexican language fluently and had a knowledge of the Mexican customs.

Owing to the secrecy of his mission, Colonel Logan wore no uniform as he travelled into Mexico with two pack mules carrying buckskin bags filled with gold. He kept his military title but used only his given name of Wentworth, a family name on his mother's side of the family tree. The same secrecy forbade the scratch of pen on paper, lest the written words be intercepted by Union forces. Therefore, he had given verbal instructions to the Negro who had accompanied him.

It was not an uncommon sight, even along the Mexican border, for a white man to have a Negro slave to do the cooking and camp chores. As they journeyed through Sonora, Mexico, the Colonel had made his mission known only to those Mexicans who held title to the old Spanish land grants. In the secret plan of the Confederacy to gain possession of Sonora by purchase or secession from Mexico, there was the veiled threat of force of arms to back up the gold in the Colonel's saddle bags.

The Colonel's son, Jeb, had left their Kentucky horse farm a few years before. The restless call to high adventure had appealed to Jeb, and it was not until he joined Quantrill's Guerrillas and found himself in such hardened outlaw company as Jesse and Frank James and Cole Younger, that Jeb realized the folly of his mistake. Jeb left the Guerrillas, rebelling at outlawry and rape, arson and cold-blooded murder.

In the first grey of dawn Jeb Logan gouged out the loose sand of the dry wash with his hands, to make a deep pit to bury the Negro. Two feet below the surface the water seeped in and Jeb watched its rising level. It had been twenty-four hours or more since he had tasted water. They had travelled the dry wash half the night where water could have been had many hours ago. Now, when he wanted a dry grave, the water came. Jeb's grating laugh had blasphemy in it as he watched his horse and mule drink. Then he heard someone say, *"Que pasá, Señor?"* The voice was sonorous, deep-toned as a bell.

The white-haired man, in rawhide sandals and a patched, faded brown priest's robe, came down from the bank behind him. As the priest looked down at the dead Negro, the deep brown eyes in the leathery face ignored the gun in Jeb's hand.

"What is the matter?" The question was repeated in the language of the north. There was no prying curiosity; only an unselfish desire to be of aid. The lean, strong brown fingers toyed with the thick white cord around the waist of the shabby brown robe.

Making a gesture towards the dead body, Jeb said, "We ran into an Apache ambush sometime after dark. The arrow went into the lung tissue. Have you ever pulled a barbed flint arrowhead from a man's flesh?" he asked.

"I have pulled out arrows and spears that went deep," the priest answered, his dark eyes clouded with memory. "The spearheads are the worst." The hands made a gesture. "Quench your thirst. Then we shall carry your companion to a high place and give him a Christian burial."

Jeb looked down at the dead Negro. "Bugler Stack," he voiced his thoughts aloud, "always wanted a military funeral. He was a bugler in the Confederate Army."

"That, too, Señor," the padre spoke quickly, "as near as possible. There are, I believe, three old muskets among the Indians who are coming with the burro pack train. They are Pimas and of a peaceful nature."

The padre looked down at the Negro's dented brass bugle shining in the early dawn, at the faded red cord, at the campaign cap. Sadness shadowed the priest's brown eyes.

"He is not of your faith, Padre," Jeb said.

"I would not be worthy of the name priest if I harboured doubt or hesitation to perform these last rites," the padre said, as he unslung a goatskin wine bag. Twisting the stopper, he held it towards Jeb, and said, "Brandy from the vineyards of Spain."

The mellow warmth of the wine was welcome in Jeb Logan's cold, empty belly.

The sun that pushed up over the broken peaks of the

8

Rincons was a brassy ball, a winter sun without warmth to take the chill from the raw wind. As the Pimas, on foot, strung out on each side of the burro train, the tinkle of a small horse bell strapped around the neck of the lead jenny came down wind. Most of the Indians wore faded cotton shirts and moccasins to cover bare feet. Some carried long sticks sharpened at the ends to prod the reluctant animals. All of them had knives but no other weapons.

Padre Juan, speaking to them in their own language, pointed to the dead man and then to a giant saguaro on a sloping ridge above the wash. The two limbs on either side of the spined cactus were to be taken for a crudely formed cross.

The grave dug, they wrapped the Negro in a couple of blankets from the padre's bedroll and carried him up the slope. Padre Juan held a cross formed by two sticks tied together as he chanted the funeral dirge. The wind, tearing at the faded brown robe, flailed it around the lean, weathered shanks of the priest and billowed the hood thrown back from his shock of snow-white hair. The sweeping current of air lashed out at the group of stolid Pimas and fanned their long black hair across dark wooden faces. It whipped the coarse grit into Jeb's eyes as he stood hatless, head bowed, while the padre read the Latin words of the burial from a buckskin-covered Bible. When the Bible closed, the four Indians fired their ancient muskets in a farewell salute.

After the burial, the string of patient little burros moved on, the Indians plodding alongside in silence. Jeb Logan saddled the blue mule and handed the bridle reins to the padre. "Bugler would want you to have his mule, Padre."

"You will find welcome at the Mission of San Xavier del Bac. The house I keep for guests is yours whenever you choose to enter. Its roof has given shelter to many men seeking haven and sanctuary—driven, hunted men, with no other place left to go. The wounded and sick have been tended there. Some who sought shelter were enemies of the Mother Church, but I made them all welcome, gave them comfort and shelter in their final hour.

"If the time ever comes when you have sore need of shelter and a friend, my house is yours. *Vaya con Dios.*"

The padre's uplifted arm made the sign of the cross. Then he mounted the big blue mule and rode away and was soon lost to sight in the wind-swept wasteland.

Jeb Logan, his old hat pulled down across his head, remembered too late that he had forgotten to thank the padre. A dry, hard lump clogged his throat. He took the canteen from his saddle horn to fill it with water but it felt heavy in his hands. Removing the metal cap, he knew, from the pungent odour, that the priest had filled the empty canteen with brandy from his wine bag.

Jeb lifted the canteen and drank a silent salutation to the man who had befriended the living and the dead. Then he mounted the dun horse and headed in the direction of Tucson.

As he rode alone in the early sunrise, the wind at his back, Jeb reread a frayed-edged letter, written by his father before he was killed.

My beloved son Jeb,

My secret mission on behalf of the Confederacy has been accomplished, a difficult and dangerous task that required utmost diplomacy, and mailed fist beneath the gloved hand. If, by the grace of God, the Confederate States of the South are victorious, Sonora will secede and break off all allegiance with Mexico to join itself to the land purchased by our country from Mexico by terms of the Gadsden Treaty.

As a reward for the success of my mission, the Confederacy has deeded to me an old Spanish Land Grant in Pimeria Alta, now Arizona Territory. The grant is called Jornada, a Spanish word meaning among other things, a day's journey.

The explorer, Francisco Vasquez de Coronado, on his vain search for the Seven Cities of Cibola, sent one of his young soldiers with an important message to the City of Mexico, and as a reward for his perilous journey the explorer promised him a grant of land to be measured by the number of leagues he covered on his first day's horseback ride. Thus, the square block of land was named La Jornada by de Coronado and at his request it was granted to the young soldier by King Philip of Spain.

10

I have placed the map showing the location of La Jornada in the old brass telescope you will remember from your boyhood days, and I am sending it to you, together with this letter, by the Negro, Bugler Stack, with whom you grew up and who has been my constant and loyal companion, enduring untold hardships and dangers of the long, tedious journey through hostile country.

God grant Bugler a safe journey and that he finds you alive and well, so that you can claim what is your heritage, should I be killed. Safe now on United States soil, I am surrounded by Yankee enemies. My only hope of escaping assassination is by way of Sonora, and I have a rendezvous tonight with an old Indian fighter who will guide me into the safety of Mexico.

Colonel Wentworth Logan was killed that night. Bugler buried him and, fearing capture, he buried the telescope in the Colonel's grave, before starting on his search for Jeb.

Jeb's eyes itched as if filled with hot sand when he thought of how his father had died. He put the letter in a pouch of the money belt he wore around his middle under his shirt. He knew he should destroy it, but it was a last message from his father and a link binding him to the promise he had made the Negro, to find the grave and avenge his father's murder.

2

WHEN JEB LOGAN rode slowly down Calle del Arroyo, the hard grey eyes under the low-pulled hat brim missed nothing as he remembered what he needed for future reference, and discarded the rest.

Tucson was filling with all manner of people who were coming to town to spend the holidays, for tomorrow was Christmas Day. Wagons and carts filled with men, women and children. Bedwagons piled high with bedding and cooking pots and feed for the animals.

Some were mounted on horses or mules, even burros. The Mexicans and Indians who travelled on foot, yielded the road with stubborn reluctance to the wagons and carts and riders. The Mexicans, in festive mood, shouted good-natured taunts to the more fortunate who were not on foot and called out with good-humoured laughter to the others who trotted beside wagons and carts or hung on behind. Bottles and goat skins filled with mescal, aguardiente and tequila were passed down. Shouted toasts were drunk. If any liquor was left in the bottles strewn along the road, the Indians picked them up and drank as they walked along in wooden-faced silence. Their black eyes revealed nothing, save a resigned bitterness and hatred for both Mexicans and the white men who had confiscated their lands and driven them onto reservations.

Calle del Arroyo was, as the name implied, no more than a wide, well-travelled dry stream bed. Jeb let his horse pick its own way and choose its own gait, as he twisted in and out of the slower moving line of one-way traffic. Half a dozen times a tipsy Mexican held a bottle or wine bag up to Jeb as he rode past. "*Salud*" the man would say and then drink without proffering the bottle. Jeb forced a grin, his eyes wary as he rode on. He was

12

not unmindful of the young Mexican girls who eyed him with sidelong glances. Giggling and chattering like magpies, they were unaware that the tall gringo understood every word. Some of it was pleasing to a man's vanity, some childish ridicule, barbed with insult. He understood the men's uncomplimentary remarks.

Jeb Logan's mouth was a grim line across his dust-powdered face, with its week's stubble of black, wiry whiskers. The Mexican War was too fresh in the minds of the older men who had been forced to lay down arms to the conquerors from the north. They showed resentment and bitter hatred that would take many generations to breed out. Jeb did not blame them. He knew what it felt like to be homeless.

He watched the Indians on foot as he rode past them. They were the more friendly Pimas and Papagos, but their resentment was every bit as strong as that of the warlike Apaches. These Indians lacked the fighting guts of the Apaches, and therein lay the only difference.

Jeb drank from the canteen as he rode along in hard-eyed, brooding silence, thankful for the padre's brandy. He cut a look upward at the cold, brassy sun that stood past the high noon mark.

There was some sort of commotion ahead and Jeb reined off to one side. The wagons and huge wheeled carretas veered off up a side street. Jeb heard the sounds of loud cursing that came out of the dust, against the wind. He rode on to see what was happening.

Two big freight wagon outfits were blocking the street. One was drawn by yoked oxen, the other was a jerkline mule freight outfit. They had met head on as they rounded the corner of the stage depot. The street was wide enough to permit the two freight outfits to pass, with plenty of margin, but the wheel hubs on each rear wagon had locked together. The oxen and mules had halted and stood tracked, chains slacked. The bull whacker and the mule skinner, blacksnake whips looped across their shoulders, walked towards each other, cursing in leather-lunged voices with each plodding step that shortened the distance. A crowd was gathering and men spewed out of the saloons, shoving and pushing, some carrying filled glasses, others bottles.

Jeb Logan sat his horse and watched the two freighters who were no longer wasting breath in shouted curses. Both men stood on wide spread legs as they wielded the blacksnakes at one another. Each had lashed the other's hat off. Bareheaded now, they ripped at the clothing. Jerkline's buckskin shirt hung in ribbons. Bull's red flannel undershirt was ripped off to bare the hair tufted barrel chest. The whips were slashing ragged rips in the grease-grimed overalls. Suspender buttons popped to let the overalls sag. So far neither lash had drawn blood.

"Show colour, you bull whacker! I got a hundred bucks says you draw the first blood!" someone in the crowd shouted.

"Have at that ox-man, Jerkline! Draw red! The sight of blood make you sick?" taunted another.

"Quit foolin' around! Your dirty hides ain't no treat lessen they're skinned off the raw meat!" another jeered.

Others joined in the taunts and ribald laughter. Goaded by the mockery, both freighters cursed the crowd as they paused for breath. Then, as if by agreement, the long lashes hissed out and cracked. Jerkline's right ear was sliced off as if by a knife. A chunk of flesh was bitten from Bull's cheek where it bulged over a quid of tobacco.

The crowd roared approval as the lashes hissed and popped and drew the blood they wanted to see. The two freighters snarled as the poppers reddened. Neither man had come untracked from the spread-legged stance. Both were blowing hard, lips peeled back from set teeth. A few onlookers who had shouted for blood turned away now. A woman screamed for someone to stop the butchering, but nobody paid her any attention. A sickening silence held the crowd now, souring the rotgut in their bellies. This was more than they had bargained for. Only a few hardened men, who had cause to hate both combatants, now relished the fight.

The distant sound of a trumpet came down wind.

"The stage coach!" shouted a big, florid-faced man in shirt-sleeves standing in the doorway of the stage depot on the corner. "Get your damned freight outfits clear of the street, Solomon!" he yelled at Solomon Warner, the general store owner. Then lifting his voice to a bellow, he motioned the Union Army officer who spurred his

14

horse through the crowd. "Major Sherwood! Have your soldiers clear the street!" he ordered.

Jeb Logan twisted sideways in his saddle to watch the blond, red-faced man in the dress uniform of an officer of the Union Army. Sherwood, despite the major's insignia, had the look of a business man dressed up as a soldier. Bathed and scrubbed and fresh from the barber shop, the trim moustache waxed and twisted, he was handsomely arrogant, despite his poor seat in the saddle. He seemed to be having trouble controlling the sleek bay cavalry horse and handling the sword in his hand at the same time as he swung the flat blade at anybody who was slow to give way. Major Sherwood, Adjutant and Provost Marshal at Camp Lowell, was an infantry officer. His pale blue eyes searched the crowd for soldiers under his command. Most of them had imbibed freely, were unarmed and in dress uniform and on the town. They responded half-heartedly to the major's shouted commands.

The mule skinner's blacksnake cracked and the major's horse reared and whirled, all but unseating its rider.

"Bull! Jerkline!" Solomon Warner called to the two freighters. "Clear the street of the wagons!" His voice had the ring of authority.

"Throw us a couple of bottles, Sol!" called Bull Sykes. "It takes likker to move them hub-locked wheels."

The trumpet, blown by a man on the driver's seat of the stage coach, sent ahead its warning to clear the streets.

Solomon Warner handed the two freighters a bottle each, with orders to get the wagons clear without delay. But they took their time lowering the contents of the bottles, and not until they were drained and smashed on the locked wagon hubs did they make a move to get them off the street.

Both freighters walked down along their teams, calling each ox and mule by name, telling them to "tighten up". The hame bells jangled, chains clanked as each freighter shouted "Tighten up! You sons of hell! Tighten up! Haw!" The two blacksnakes cracked and popped like exploding fire crackers and there was the loud thudding crash as one hub rolled heavily over the hub of the other wagon, before breaking away.

Wagon wheels creaked in the dust. The trumpet blared

and the Butterfield Overland stage, with the six-horse team travelling at a dead run, suddenly appeared. The driver sat his seat, legs braced as the whiplash popped above the horse's heads. The trumpeter, horn lifted and blowing, sat his seat precariously beside the driver who squinted into the dust cloud ahead.

The freight wagons moved slowly apart, oxen and mules pulling the piled high freight for Solomon Warner's General Store. One rear wheel on each tail wagon looked dished-in on the splintered wagon spokes that centred in badly cracked hubs.

Both freighters stood close together now, calculating with bloodshot eyes the space left open for the heavy stage coach to pass through.

"What you think, Jerkline?" Bull Sykes shouted in the mule skinner's torn ear.

"Far enough, Bull, if that damn stage driver lives up to his braggin'."

They hollered "Whoa!" at the same time. Oxen and mules halted. "Ease off!" They stepped back a pace to slack the taut chains. "Slack up!"

Both men measured the cleared space with their whip-lashes, grimaced and nodded their approval, then walked back a safe distance to watch the fun.

There was barely enough space between the wagons for the stage coach to pass without wrecking. Bull whacker and mule skinner were now united against a common enemy. All stage drivers held freighters in contempt and lost no occasion to give profane voice to their sentiments. Bull and Jerkline stood side by side against the front wall of the adobe store.

"You drunken, misbegotten sons of hell!" Solomon Warner spoke without heat. "You carry things too far." He uncorked one bottle and handed it to the pair. "If that stage coach wrecks, they'll sue me for damages."

"We measured 'er, Sol. Let that high-chinned stage driver live up to his rep. A man gets fed up with his braggin'," Jerkline said.

Major Sherwood was having a hard time sitting his restive horse as it pranced and side-stepped and snorted, fighting its head against the tight reined bit. Sherwood tried to call out to the stage driver, whose whiplash was popping, but the wind tore the ineffectual warning from his open mouth.

"God Almighty!" the big man in the doorway of the stage depot said, gripping the jamb on either side till the knuckles showed white. There was more of a prayer than blasphemy in the whispered words.

Jeb Logan stiffened in his saddle as he saw the buckled-down side curtain of the Concord coach open and a woman's head and face appear.

The dust had settled enough for the stage driver to see the two stalled freight outfits that blocked the street. His leg stiffened against the high brake as he tightened the six lines, his narrowed eyes gauging the scant opening a hundred feet ahead. The lead team slacked their running pace and tightened the tugs as the buckskin lash cracked. The trumpeter gripped the seat with both hands. The girl quickly pulled in her head.

The six horses tore through the opening at a dead run. There was the heavy, sickening crash as the coach swung and rocked on leather springs and hit a front wheel against one of the wagons, splintering the spokes into kindling wood. The axle on the driver's side scraped the ground. The iron tyre rolled like a loop, smashing through the crowd. The stage driver, catapulted into the air, arms and legs flailing, let go the lines and whip. The trumpeter was thrown clear.

Jeb Logan spurred his horse as the runaway team, dragging the crippled coach, headed in his direction. Angling his course so that he came up alongside the coach and the swing team, he leaned out to grab the lines fastened to the bits of the lead team.

In the military plaza ahead he saw the crowd scatter and run as he sawed on the taut lines in an effort to circle the horses in a wide arc around the open plaza. Dripping sweat and blowing as the crippled coach threatened to turn over, the horses, badly winded, slowed down and stopped almost in front of the stage depot.

The big man, who had stood paralyzed in the doorway, stumbled out into the street, the soggy, chewed-down cigar clamped in the corner of his mouth. His big hair-tufted hands tore the heavy canvas curtains apart as he sobbed in desperate, frantic haste, "Mona! Mona!"

The girl's laugh was a little off-key, high-pitched with a sob caught in it. The big man lifted her out in his arms, holding her in a bear hug that took her off her feet. Then he let her down.

Jeb sat his horse, his weight in one stirrup, and stared with frank boldness at the girl, whose poke bonnet hung down her back over tangled dark red hair. The colour had not yet come back into her face and the dozen freckles across her nose and cheek bones showed darkly against the ivory white of her skin. Her heavily lashed eyes were the colour of sage after a rain, her body long and slender, full breasted, in the dark grey dress. Her eyes met the bold stare of Jeb Logan.

"I want to thank you," Major Sherwood was saying to Jeb Logan, "on behalf of my fiancée." He had somehow managed to dismount before being thrown. He slapped some of the yellow dust from the new blue uniform, and a frown of annoyance showed on his flushed face when Jeb paid him no attention whatever.

In stopping the runaway team the lines had burned through Jeb's shabby gauntlet gloves, leaving raw welts on his hands and fingers. He was pulling off the gloves as his eyes and the girl's met and held. He felt the pounding pulse beat in his throat and a faint, almost sardonic smile twisted his cracked lips.

He realized what he must look like with the stubble of black whiskers and red lidded, bloodshot eyes, the uncut wiry black hair, the old sweat-marked hat and dirty grey flannel shirt, the shabby brush jacket and scarred leather chaps. Horse and rider were dust powdered from head to foot and showed marks of the long trail ride.

Major Sherwood's was a natural mistake as he sized the rider up for a border renegade. "Have yourself a time," said the Major, his voice stern, yet tolerant, as he handed a couple of bank notes up to Jeb.

It is doubtful whether Jeb heard. If so, he gave no sign. His attention was centred on the girl.

Sherwood was livid with rage. He stepped forward and jerked at the loose bridle reins of Jeb's horse. Jeb twisted in the saddle with the swift, unbroken ease of a horseman, and for the first time took notice of the well-kept hand that shoved the money at him.

"I'm Major Sherwood from Camp Lowell," he introduced himself, his voice brittle. "Here's some money. Finish out your drunk in the saloons. Satisfy your lusts in Maiden Lane." He shoved the money up along the horse's withers.

Jeb Logan looked down into the anger-flushed, arrogant face. Contemptuously he sized the Major up from cap to polished boots. Then he reached down and took the bank notes, tore them in half and let a gust of wind carry them away. "I'm Captain Jeb Logan, late of Quantrill's Confederate Cavalry," he said from behind teeth bared in a wolfish grin. Jeb leaned from his saddle and the gauntlet glove made a flat sound as it slapped against the Major's barbered face.

"I'll be easy to find, Yankee," Jeb said flatly, "if you care to take up the challenge." He dropped the old glove at the Major's boots, then reined his horse so that the Major was forced to step back quickly to avoid being ridden down.

As Jeb rode past the girl standing beside the grey-haired man, he lifted his hat. When their eyes met, he gave her a crooked grin. As he rounded the corner of El Camino Real, he heard a rebel yell in the crowd, and the welcome, friendly, defiant sound of it widened the grin on his face.

When he reached the compound where he had seen horses and mules, he dismounted and was reaching for the latigo strap to undo the saddle cinch when a voice with a southern drawl sounded behind him.

"I'd be proud to shake the hand and salute the glove that slapped the face of that pompous damn yankee." The words came jerkily, pantingly, as if the man had been running to overtake the horsebacker.

Jeb Logan saw a small, wiry man with weathered skin that crinkled when he grinned. He was holding out his hand and saying, "Robert N. Leatherwood from the Confederate Army of North Carolina, at your service, Suh. Allow me the honour of being your second in case Major Sherwood has the guts to pick up the gauntlet. It's high time somebody cut that overbearin' braggart down to size."

"I lost my temper," Jeb said, his hot anger already cooling as he shook hands. "I'm Jeb Logan from Kentucky. I

19

guess I spoke out of turn when I admitted I rode with Quantrill's Guerrillas."

A scowl fought the grin on Leatherwood's face. "That damn yankee will use the information, Logan, no doubt about that. Let's walk that dun horse of yours up the arroyo to my stables. My house hasn't much to offer in the way of hospitality, but such as it is it's your home as long as you stay in Tucson."

As they approached the stables, Jeb could see that it was quite a layout. Eight foot adobe walls surrounded the place and over the door hung a rustic sign—ROBERT N. LEATHERWOOD'S STABLES.

When the horse had been cared for and Bob Leatherwood produced a bottle, Jeb inquired about the red-haired lady in the stage coach.

"Matt Durand's daughter, Mona," Bob answered. "Her father is manager of the Butterfield Overland Stage Line. A two-bottle man and cunning as a fox, cold-blooded in any kind of game or land grabbin' deal. He'd grin in your face while he shot you in the briskit or spilled your guts on the floor with a Bowie knife. Matt Durand holds options on half the old Spanish land grants in Arizona Territory. His daughter is his sole heir. Mona has just come from school in California."

"The yankee Major said she was his fiancé, Bob," Jeb said.

"Could be. Sherwood transferred here from Fort Stockton, California. His old man is a California Senator with wealth and power enough to get that bald-faced dude a Major's commission." Leatherwood made a wry face, and added, "It all adds up in Matt's book."

Bob Leatherwood filled their empty glasses and said, "Let's likker, Jeb. Then I'll take you to Solomon Warner's store for new clothes and then supper at California Mary's in Maiden Lane. Best grub in town with imported French champagne. Five will get you fifty none of it will cost you a shin plaster. You're a hero, Jeb. An hour from now there will be a hundred and one versions of that little drama with the stage coach. Lawdy, man," he exclaimed, "like a three act play it was. The two freighters, the runaway coach and the rescue, the challenge to a duel. Why, that California yankee will have to fight or get laughed out of Arizona." Leatherwood lifted his drink, and said, "Here's luck to you, Jeb Logan." They clicked glasses.

Before they left the cabin Bob Leatherwood took a Confederate grey uniform and cap from his trunk and laid them out on the bunk. "Tomorrow," he announced with waspish pride, "is Christmas Day. I'll dress up and we'll make the rounds."

The Civil War had ended a dozen years or more, but on state occasions Leatherwood would don his Confederate uniform and with the grey cap at a fighting slant, the banty-sized little man, shouting the rebel yell in saloons and brothels, strutted down the streets of the crumbling walled old Pueblo of Tucson. No man had the temerity to check Bob Leatherwood in his cocky stride. Tucson as a whole was proud of the little rebel, who was destined to leave his mark in Arizona Territory. His fiery speeches, his love for horses were becoming legend.

3

Bob Leatherwood seemed to be correct in his premise that Jeb Logan had attained a certain unique distinction, but the fiery little rebel was stretching it a little when he said Jeb would be proclaimed a hero.

Time was when Tucson and Arizona Territory had been in strong sympathy with the cause for which the Southern Confederacy had fought. Captain Sherod Hunter and his Texan Confederate Cavalry had found a hearty welcome awaiting their arrival and for a few brief months, while the Confederate flag was raised in Tucson, the inhabitants were loyal, and men volunteered for enlistment. But when Captain Hunter left and the Union forces from California moved in, it was another story. No rebel shouts were heard as men rode along El Camino Real. The Union flag whipped in the wind as the sun and rain faded its colours. Tucson was under Military Law. The Californians, bitter and resentful, fine-combed the town for Confederate sympathizers. Not a day passed but what some luckless man was tied to the whipping post while the Union soldiers did the lashing. Fear of the Union flag suppressed the citizenry.

Solomon Warner who had fled to Sonora, Mexico, when Captain Hunter told him to "take up arms and join the Confederate Army or get the hell out", had returned after the invasion of the Californians. Shrewd, tough as a boot, he freighted in supplies by pack mule and wagon to restock his general store.

Jeb Logan was no Confederate hero in the hard, shrewdly humorous eyes of Solomon Warner, who bore no love for the Confederacy and its lost cause. A big man in every way, he was too clever in a business way to voice resentment, but he had written letters to Washington, listing his claims for damages suffered at the hands of the Confederate Army.

Solomon Warner was angling for a Government contract to freight supplies to Camp Lowell on the outskirts of Tucson. Right now both oxen and mule freight wagons were loaded with army supplies freighted across the desert from Fort Yuma on the Colorado River.

"This is Jeb Logan, Sol," Bob Leatherwood introduced Jeb. "He's come a long ways and needs outfittin' from hat to boots. The best you got in the store." Bob grinned and winked, saying, "Jeb Logan saved your bacon, Sol, when he kept the stage team from being crippled. Matt Durand would have sued you from hell to breakfast if they'd been hurt. You can charge Jeb's outfit to good will."

Solomon Warner, a faint smile on his bearded mouth that never reached his eyes, looked down at the jockey-sized Leatherwood. "I figured when you came in, Leatherwood, you'd come to pay your bill to start the new year square with the world." Warner seemed to be taking a dim view of things.

"I'll pay you on New Year's Eve, Sol, one minute before midnight. Have my bill made out and I'll have the money in my hand. You can mark the bill paid if you've learned to spell the word. Last time it was spelled P-A-D-E."

Warner had given Jeb Logan the benefit of a long scrutiny without offering his hand.

"I'll pay for what I get, Warner," Jeb's flat-toned voice put a damper on the rough banter. "Trot out the best you have."

"No need to get riled up, Logan," Warner said, his big rough hands making a gesture. "Me and this gamecock rebel goes at it hammer and tongs. Neither of us would have it any different. Help yourself to what's in stock."

Solomon Warner closed the front door and brought out a bottle of bonded whisky from under the counter, and some clean glasses. He poured the drinks and handed each man a glass, lifting his own in a salute.

"Matt will bill me for plenty damages," Solomon said, "for wrecking the Concord coach. He'll blame it on that whip fight those two drunk freighters of mine put on."

Then looking at Jeb Logan, he said, "If I was in your boots, I'd walk careful and speak easy, Logan."

"You wouldn't be trying to throw a scare into me?"

"Hell, no. You don't look like you'd scare easy. Just a friendly warnin'. Major Sherwood throws a lot of weight around here."

"That damn yankee Californian will either fight," Leatherwood chuckled, "or tuck his coyote tail between his legs and run."

"That remains to be seen, Leatherwood," said Warner. Then to Jeb Logan he said, "Pick out a hat from that new shipment I just got from Philadelphia, Logan. Compliments of Sol Warner. Like the little rebel says, I owe you somethin'." The eyes that had squinted along rifle sights to get a bead on more than a few Apaches held a twinkle as he poured the whisky for a second drink.

Half an hour and another drink, Leatherwood and Logan left, each carrying a big bundle down the street to the barber shop.

Half a dozen unshaven customers were waiting. Leatherwood knew them all by name as he introduced Jeb Logan, who was already known by sight and reputation.

"If you boys got nothin' but time to waste," Leatherwood grinned down the line of waiting men, "me'n Jeb's in a hell of a rush. Jeb wants to be scrubbed and barbered and freshly dressed when he fights the pistol duel." The words left a hushed silence.

"You mean the Major took it up?" one of them asked in a whisper.

"I'm waitin' word from his seconds any minute," Leatherwood lied glibly. "I'm actin' for Jeb Logan."

The man lying back in the barber chair sat up, his face lathered to the cheek bones. He pulled the apron from around his neck saying, "Take my turn." A pair of hard steel-grey eyes showed above the lather. "Good luck, Jeb Logan," he said as he held out a calloused hand. "Give Logan the works, Manuel," he told the Mexican barber. "It's on Pete Kitchen." Then selecting a razor from the wall case, Kitchen stood on wide-spread legs and finished shaving without benefit of mirror.

As Jeb leaned back, bibbed and lathered, he listened to the talk that buzzed around him. He prided himself as a Southerner that he could hold his liquor with any man, but he felt a little dizzy as he lay back with closed eyes. He was in need of sleep and hot food, and as the steaming hot towel covered his face and he fought back the urge to take five in the barber chair, the words of the Negro came back: "When he lit a sulphur match I saw his eyes, like steel they was, the colour of a gun barrel. A kinda stocky built man, with an old Mexican serape across his shoulders, a carbine in the crook of his elbow. He kinda bit off his words. You'll know who killed yo' pappy, Cap'n Jeb, by them steely eyes and the way he's got of spittin' out every word."

Jeb Logan came awake with his gun in his hand under the long apron and almost fell out of the chair.

"Hold it, Jeb," Bob Leatherwood chuckled. "Hold steady till Manuel shears you."

Jeb saw the shame-faced grin on his clean shaven face in the mirror. Reflected there were all the men who were waiting, save one. Pete Kitchen had finished shaving and gone out.

The wind had died down with the setting sun as Jeb and Bob made their way through the motley holiday crowd to Ojito Springs. There they found a big blackened boiler full of water heating on a bed of mesquite coals and tubs in a row of bath houses.

Removing a wide buckskin money belt, the pouches bulging, Jeb stripped to the hide. He laid the money belt and his two guns and cartridge belt within easy reach as a Mexican boy poured buckets of steaming hot water into the tub. Then he eased himself in and soaked. Scrubbing his body with a long-handled stiff brush, he listened to the voices in the thin-walled bath houses around him. The talk was profane and tipsy as they shouted their opinions of the whip fight, the runaway and the outcome of the inevitable duel between the stranger on the dun horse and the Major.

Bob Leatherwood was waiting for Jeb when he came out. He pursed his lips in a tuneless whistle. "I'd give a purty if that red headed Mona Durand was here to see what she looked down her nose at," he said.

"But she ain't here," Jeb answered, flushed and ill at ease under the banter.

"Hell, no. She's at the officers' ball at Camp Lowell with Major Sherwood. We weren't invited, so we'll like as not wind up at sunrise at some Mexican *baile* and sober up on big bowls of *menuda*. But lawdy man, the grub we'll sit down to at California Mary's an hour from now will be something to remember."

The exuberance of the little rebel was contagious as he led the way to Maiden Lane. The hot bath had steamed all aches and pains of fatigue from Jeb's weary body. He was sober and hungry and clean and ready to go along with Bob Leatherwood when he vowed they'd paint the town.

The grin left Jeb's barbered face when he remembered the Negro in his unmarked grave. Jeb and Bugler Stack had grown up together and back home they had called the Negro Jeb's black shadow. Bugler would want it this way, regardless, Jeb thought.

"Somebody walkin' across your grave, Jeb?" asked Leatherwood, who noticed the dark look clouding the face of his companion.

"The grave belongs to a man who died last night. Padre Juan gave him a Christian burial at sunrise. The man was a Negro, a boyhood companion in Kentucky. We ran the gauntlet of some Apaches after dark. Bugler got an arrow in his back. I was thinking about him when you spoke, knowing he'd sort of like me to celebrate."

4

A HUGE Christmas tree with tinsel and bright coloured ornaments and candles reached the ceiling in the front parlour of California Mary's. Piles of wrapped gifts banked the base of the tree.

California Mary was a handsome woman, dressed in a formal gown, as were all her girls, known as "grey doves", who stood with her to greet the callers.

A score or more men were lined at the bar. All were dressed in their Sunday best. If a swear word slipped out by accident the offender was jabbed roughly by thumb or elbow. All had checked their guns with their hats in the entrance hall.

The long dining-room table was stacked from end to end with large platters of roast wild turkey, venison and antelope; mashed white and sweet potatoes; bowls of cranberry sauce; mince pies and rounded plum puddings corraled by the blue flames of burning brandy.

The jockey-sized Bob Leatherwood never left his tall, dark-haired companion's side. "It's a privilege and an honour to introduce Captain Jeb Logan of the Confederate Cavalry," he'd say, leaving out all reference to Quantrill's Guerrillas. But every one present, including California Mary and her girls, were aware that Jeb Logan had been one of that hard riding outfit.

He, of course, could have been among the ones who had dissented and broken off affiliation with Quantrill when he had given his men the privilege of leaving or staying after General Lee's surrender. There was whispered discussion among the tight groups of men at the bar, but no man had the temerity to come out point blank with it. Something in Jeb's eyes forbade questioning and he offered no hint or word by way of clearing

27

up the unspoken question. There were too many men here who had been Union sympathizers, a sprinkling of men who had worn the Union blue, others who had been in sympathy with the Southern cause and had now taken the oath of allegiance. From time to time Leatherwood, speaking in an undertone, pointed them out.

Jeb Logan, a stranger, was made to feel it. Now and then a man smiled faintly or winked an eye as he shook hands. A few of the tipsy guests wished him luck if and when Major Sherwood had the guts to fight a pistol duel. One or two voiced the same warning and quiet advice, to watch his step, given Jeb by Solomon Warner.

Jeb's muscles tightened across his cold belly as he looked at each man with a thin smile, his eyes wary, so that he would remember each face again if they met under different circumstances. He kept his back to the wall as much as possible. His eyes, restless under heavy black brows, kept searching for a glimpse of Pete Kitchen, but the tough Indian fighter was nowhere to be seen. When the time was right, Jeb meant to question Bob Leatherwood about Kitchen.

"You have the lean look of a hungry man," the woman's voice beside him was low in tone and vibrant with an intriguing huskiness.

When Jeb turned to look at her, she seemed to move closer against him, so that her eyes were almost on a level with his, her soft breath touching his face. She was a tall, beautiful girl with large breasts, in a honey-coloured low-cut evening gown that matched the shade of her hair and the eyes he was looking into.

There was a challenge in the light brown, yellow flecked eyes, an invitation in the full red lipped mouth, a subtle mockery in the faint smile. "Let's eat, Captain Jeb Logan," she said softly, sliding a bare arm possessively through the crook of his elbow. It all happened with a lithe smoothness in the space of a few seconds as she led him away from the crowded bar through an alcove into the dining room.

Jeb, aware of the hushed silence that had stilled the voices of the men at the bar, was conscious of the open staring of everyone. "I'll be around when you need me, Jeb," he heard Bob Leatherwood say quietly.

The girl picked up two china plates from the stack and started down the long table. White-jacketed waiters piled both plates high with all the silver platters had to offer. "We'll eat in privacy, if it won't embarrass you, Captain," she said, the smile on her lips touching her eyes as she turned away and let him follow.

Her silk dress was a tight sheath fitting her uncorseted body as she moved with a smooth litheness. When they came to a door at the far end of the hall, she handed the plates to Jeb and unlocked the door.

Candles in a silver candelabra were burning on a round table covered with a white linen cloth. The table was set for two. Chilled bottles of champagne, whisky and brandy stood on a sideboard. The room was furnished in excellent taste, with upholstered furniture and Brussels carpeting. A fire burned in the open grate. The room had a genteel simplicity, and through the curtained alcove Jeb saw the bedroom.

Jeb placed the plates on the table while the girl snapped the heavy lock on the door. There was a mocking smile that barely parted the full ripe lips of her mouth. Her flecked eyes reflected the flickering candle light.

Blood pulsing into his throat, Jeb took her in his arms and felt the willowy body melt into his as his mouth closed over her lips. Then her hands pushed him away and she glided past him across the room to the sideboard. The neck of the decanter rattled against the two tall glasses as she poured whisky into them. When she handed Jeb his, holding her own in a hand that trembled slightly, she said, "I want you to know, Jeb, that I am not one of California Mary's 'grey doves'. My name is Fay Wayne, a stage name. Major Sherman Sherwood pays my room rent here. Nobody but California Mary knows that I am his mistress and he has the only key to this door." Her upper lip curled back in more of a feline snarl than a smile.

"It was Major Sherwood who paid my stage coach fare from Fort Stockton, California." She gulped her drink, choking a little. "I was within earshot when he thanked you in behalf of his fiancée Mona Durand." She spat the name out like a bitter taste and finished her drink. "And that," she finished bitterly, "was news to me, his common law wife. I was here a week before I found out

29

that I was living in a sporting house, where he'd brought me." She splashed whisky into a glass and the edge of the glass rattled against her teeth. Her short laugh was brittle. "I don't believe Sherwood has the guts to fight a pistol duel, but if he does, I want to be there to watch you kill him for the kind of a slimy thing he is."

They touched glasses and drank as their eyes met and held. He held her chair and kissed her when she was seated. He opened the champagne and filled their glasses. Jeb tried not to wolf his food. She laughed softly when his plate was bare. "You were hungry, Jeb," she said, leaning across the table to blow out the candles.

There was only the dull red glow of mesquite coals when Jeb lifted her in his arms. Dawn was greying the sky outside the shuttered windows when a rap sounded on the door.

"We have a warrant for the arrest of a Quantrill outlaw by the name of Jeb Logan," the nasal whisky-thick voice came through the door. "Open up. We got orders to shoot if you resist arrest."

Jeb shoved his money belt into the hands of the girl. "Keep this," he said. "Find Bob Leatherwood. He'll get you a room somewhere. Get out of here as quickly as you can. I'll get these damn yankees away." He held her close for a moment, kissing her hard.

Fully dressed, Jeb entered the living room and found that the Union soldiers were already in the apartment. He was looking into the black muzzles of six rifles with fixed bayonets in the hands of the soldiers.

"Face the wall," barked a soldier with sergeant chevrons on his blue sleeve, "unless you want your guts spilled on the carpet. Tie his hands, men. Run him through if he makes a wrong move. Search him."

Jeb eyed them with cold contempt as he faced the wall and put both hands behind his back. There was a deadliness to his silent calm obedience to the harsh commands. He was unarmed, having left his gun with his hat in the main entrance hall.

The soldiers marched him out. The sergeant, a lewd grin on his bloated face, locked the door and held the apartment key palmed in his big hand. Then he put Major Sherwood's key in his pocket.

Two squads of soldiers with fixed bayonets surrounded the whipping post in the Military Plaza on the other side of Calle del Arroyo. As they marched past Leatherwood's stables, Jeb saw no light in Bob's house and none of the Mexican stable hands were around. But his eyes narrowed when he sighted Major Sherwood standing in the background.

"Strip him to the waist," Sherwood ordered in a flat tone. "Tie him up by the thumbs till he stretches. Fifty lashes, Sergeant. I'll do the counting."

Two men ripped his new flannel shirt to shreds. A wet rawhide thong tightened around both thumbs. The rope, looped into the thongs, tightened, and he was pulled up until his boot heels lifted from the hard packed ground.

Jeb gritted his teeth as the lash drew blood. He twisted his head till he could see Major Sherwood counting behind him. "You yellow-gutted damn yankee," Jeb's teeth bared in a mirthless grin. "I'll remember every lash when the time comes."

Fouling the air with obscenities Major Sherwood said, his face livid with fury, "You'll have time enough to think it over while you rot in Fort Yuma Prison."

Jeb did not see the girl on horseback until she almost rode him down, a white-faced girl with a tangle of dark red hair, dressed in a green divided skirt and buckskin jacket. She rode past Sherwood and lashed her riding crop back and forth across the small bloodshot eyes and the sweat-beaded red face of the sergeant doing the whipping. Then she leaned over and slashed the rope that tied Jeb with a long-bladed Bowie knife.

Jeb had to brace his legs to keep from falling. There was a twisted grin on his mouth as he held up both hands with the swollen thumbs for her to cut the rawhide that was embedded deep into the flesh. As his swollen, lacerated thumbs were freed, his right hand closed over her hand that held the knife. His lips twisted in a ghastly grin when he said, "You've paid your debt, lady. I'm grateful."

There was in the depths of Mona Durand's eyes a bright spark of excitement and something else that went deeper to hold his pain-squinted stare. Her hand slid over his as her fingers closed his grip on the knife. Then her faint smile was gone, and she reined the big, sweat-wet bay horse away. It was the same horse that had given Major Sherwood trouble the previous afternoon.

Jeb's ripped, blood-smeared naked torso and sweat-matted head, made a grim picture as he held the girl's knife in his hand. A considerable crowd had gathered and the crimson sunrise shed a red glow through the dust haze. The circle of soldiers surrounding the whipping post had their rifles gripped, the naked steel of the polished bayonets keeping the crowd back.

Jeb cut a look at the beefy sergeant, both hands across his bruised, swollen eyes, the bullwhip, with its sodden red lash, at his feet. Jeb walked slowly across the fifty feet of ground between himself and Major Sherwood, who was unfastening the holster flap that held his service revolver in place. The colour had drained from his red face, leaving the skin putty coloured.

The rattle of wheels and the jingle of chain tugs sounded as the mule-drawn buckboard rounded the corner of the stage depot but the crowd paid it no attention, their collective gaze fixed on the grim, blood-ripped Jeb Logan with the knife in his hand. Bob Leatherwood in his grey Confederate uniform, his cap at a rakish angle, handled the lines. Alongside him sat Matt Durand, his huge bulk dwarfing Leatherwood, whose voice lifted in a wild rebel yell. Matt's beefy face was mottled, his teeth clamped down on the dead cigar in the corner of his mouth, as he braced his legs in an attempt to hang on to the seat.

"Heads up!" someone yelled. "The Johnny rebs are takin' over!"

The crowd scattered like quail. The thin line of soldiers, with levelled guns and fixed bayonets, wavered, hesitated, then left. Three or four soldiers, knocked down by the mule team, screamed muffled curses in the dust cloud.

Bob Leatherwood sawed on the lines, one leg rigid on the brake. He pulled the mules back on their haunches between Jeb Logan and Major Sherwood, and dropped the lines. His hands came up with a sawed-off double-barrelled shotgun he had been sitting on.

"Talk fast, Matt," Leatherwood shouted loud enough to be heard by the crowd that now filled the clearing around the whipping post. "Talk fast and talk straight, or, by God, you'll see the damndest slaughter of yankee tin soldiers a man ever witnessed." The shotgun prodded Matt until he stood up.

Matt was bareheaded. His short-tailed nightshirt was half tucked into his pants. His bare feet were shoved in a pair of old red carpet slippers. Pouches hung under the bloodshot eyes as he stabbed a forefinger at Major Sherwood. "You tell them damn soldiers to stack arms in the plaza and get the hell back to quarters," he growled. "And hereafter you confine your activities within the boundaries of Camp Lowell. It's time you learned that Tucson has its own civil government. Military law in Tucson has ended. If I were in your boots, Sherwood, I'd march well in the lead of your men, because no one is going to lift a finger to stop Jeb Logan from carving you up. That whipping post is a thing of the past. Chop it down!"

Matt Durand was puffing. Cold sweat beaded his jowled face. He looked down at Bob Leatherwood. "That satisfy you, Leatherwood?" he asked, his eyes glinting.

"Hoist your big carcass outa my rig, Matt." Leatherwood grinned when he said it. "Ride home in one of your stage coaches or walk. It ain't more'n a mile back to your house."

Matt heaved his big hulk over the cramped front wheel onto the ground.

"Climb in, Jeb," Bob Leatherwood invited. "I'm takin' you to the vet's." His puckered eyes had a bleak look.

As they drove down the street Leatherwood pulled up in front of Solomon Warner's store, where the storekeeper stood framed in the doorway.

"Fetch out the best shirt you got, Sol," Bob told him.

When Sol brought the shirt out, he said, "Take my advice and leave town, Logan." He walked away.

"Swing past California Mary's, Bob," Jeb said. "I left my hat and guns there. Could be we'll pick up a passenger."

"A lady, I hope," said Leatherwood.

"A lady, Bob."

"I got wind of what was comin', Jeb, so I got Matt outa bed. Mona heard me talkin' to her father and before we left, she saddled that bay horse the Major borrowed yesterday and left in a hurry. I got here as quick as I could, but too late."

"Thirty-seven lashes too late, Bob."

"I got the finest and biggest stock of horse medicine and salves in the Territory. A week-ten days I'll have your back healed."

"All but the scars, Bob. Somebody's going to pay double for every one of the thirty-seven lashes."

"Amen to that. And good huntin'."

While Bob went in the main doorway of California Mary's, to pick up Jeb's hat and six-shooters, Jeb knocked on the door of Fay's room. When there was no answer, he turned the knob and went in through the unlocked door. There was no trace left of the girl. Her clothes and trunk were gone.

"I reckon the girl's at your house, Bob," Jeb told Leatherwood when he came back to the rig and put on his hat and buckled on his cartridge belt, examining the holstered guns.

They circled around and came in by way of the cemetery road. Bob left the mule team at the stable and told the Mexican to saddle his horse and Jeb's line-backed dun.

Bob's adobe cabin was empty. There was no note to indicate the girl had been there. Leatherwood bathed Jeb's back with a strong carbolic solution that stung and burned, then rubbed gall cure salve deep in the lash welts.

Leatherwood left Jeb at the cabin to wash up while he went up the street to find out what he could about the girl. He was gone an hour and ten minutes by the clock. When he returned, his mouth had a grim set and his eyes smouldered with cold anger.

"She left by stage coach at six o'clock, bag and baggage, California bound. You know who she is, Jeb?"

"Yeah. I know. But you tell me what you found out."

"She was Major Sherwood's private stock. An actress from Fort Stockton, California, named Fay Wayne. That drunk sergeant spread the news, showing the Major's key to her apartment to the crowd and broadcasting the details. Get your hat, Jeb, we're travellin'."

Leatherwood buckled on his gun belt and put some jars of salve and tins of powder into saddle bags, along with two quarts of corn liquor and a couple of pairs of clean socks. Jeb smiled thinly as he remembered the money belt he had given the girl. He did not feel any regret over the loss of the money, but the way things stood it looked as if Fay Wayne had played him for a sucker.

Jeb had found a leather sheath among Bob's trappings in the lean-to shed where he hung harness and saddles. He was fitting the Bowie knife into it, sliding it back and forth to shape the blade to the stiff saddle leather scabbard, and wondering how a girl like Mona Durand happened to be in possession of a man's knife. Apparently the knife had seen hard usage, as there were seven deep notches filed on the staghorn handle. Holding it to the light he could see the lettering that was etched on the brass guard between handle and blade. He spelled out each letter aloud: *T O N D R O.*

"Tondro!" Bob Leatherwood's head jerked around from where he was buckling the straps on his saddle bags. A puzzled frown pulled his eyebrows together.

"It's the name on this Bowie knife Mona Durand used to cut me loose," Jeb said. "Sounds Injun."

"It's the name of a cold-blooded killer," Bob said, his eyes hard with memory. "Let me see that knife, Jeb."

Holding the knife in his hands, Bob scrutinized each small detail, the worn, hard-used look, the seven notches, the name. He broke off a long black hair from a braided horsehair rope coiled on a wooden peg, and drew the whetted honed blade across it, severing the hair and repeating the act several times.

"Tondro bragged about shaving with his Bowie knife," said Bob. "And about using it to scalp the men he killed, collecting bounty on each scalp." He ran a thumbnail slowly along the seven notches, his eyes slivered. "I can name six of these notches, Jeb. They were all owners of Spanish land grants in what is now Arizona Territory by benefit of the Gadsden Purchase."

Jeb stood rigid, tense, scarcely breathing lest he interrupt the speaker.

"One of the notches," Leatherwood went on, "I have no name for, but I reckon Pete Kitchen could supply it. Pete took Tondro's trail into Sonora, Mexico, when he quit the country, but when Pete came back alone in a month or more he had nothing to say."

Leatherwood's voice was vibrant as he held the knife in the palm of his calloused hand and said, "I'd shore give somethin' to know how come Mona Durand got hold of this knife. Tondro's the only one who's supposed to have handled this knife. Why, he even slept with it in his hand." Bob handed the knife back to Jeb.

"The story goes," Bob continued talking, "that Tondro was employed by Matt Durand and his California partner, Senator Sherwood, to wipe out all heirs and owners to old Spanish land grants in Pimeria Alta. But the story would take a hell of a lot of proof to back it up in any law court."

"What you're talking about, Bob," Jeb said, "ties in with what fetched me here. If the Negro were here, he might name one of those notches on Tondro's scalping knife. The Negro was here some years ago and came back with me as a guide to show me an unmarked grave. That's all I can tell you right now, Bob." Jeb Logan's lips tightened before he talked too much.

"I'm asking no questions, Jeb," said Bob. "But you're packin' your own death warrant when you carry Tondro's knife."

"I know, Bob. Maybe we better split up here. I'm heading for trouble."

Bob Leatherwood shoved out a hand and Jeb Logan felt the steel grip of his fingers.

"If you're headin' for trouble, Jeb," Bob's face wrinkled in a grin that puckered his hard bright eyes, "Robert N. Leatherwood's goin' along for the horseback ride. There's time for a quick drink, then we'll get the hell gone while the trail's open."

5

EL CAMINO REAL, the Royal Highway, followed the Santa Cruz River the length of its fertile valley, with the Tucson Mountains to the West and the Rincons to the East, the Santa Catalina range to the North and the Santa Ritas to the South, and the Altar range farther South across the Mexican border.

The wide road, rutted by heavy freight wagons, formed a drab, twisting ribbon against the high grass. Giant old cottonwood trees, their limbs skeleton bare at this season, marked the course of the river, widened in places by beaver dams.

As Jeb Logan and Bob Leatherwood reined up to let their horses drink at Silver Lake along the way, the sound of the old Spanish bell at the Mission San Xavier del Bac came faintly on the morning breeze from the West.

"If you like, we could swing past the Mission for breakfast," said Bob Leatherwood.

Jeb, half sick with pain, felt no pangs of hunger, but he wanted to see the white-haired padre, and said so. Bob had told Jeb there was an old map at the Mission showing the Spanish land grants in Pimeria Alta, and the location of those land grants had much to do with Jeb's being here, especially the one called *La Jornada*.

Remembering now that his father's letter was in the money belt he had given Fay Wayne, he cursed himself inwardly for not having destroyed it. Should it fall into wrong hands, the letter would reveal too much, but there was no use bemoaning the loss now. No one but himself knew that the map and deed to La Jornada were inside the big brass telescope in the unmarked grave of his father in Madera Canyon. He'd ask Leatherwood later where he could locate the canyon.

As they topped a rise that rounded a small hill, they had a panoramic view of the picturesque Mission, around which milled hundreds of Indians, their faces streaked with war paint and all armed with long spears and bows and arrows. Some of the Indians wore breech clouts, others wore faded cotton jeans and cotton shirts. One half-naked Pima, his arms flailing the air as he made some kind of speech, stood on top of a small knoll in front of a large wooden cross.

"Somethin's wrong," Bob Leatherwood said, sliding his Winchester from the saddle scabbard. Jeb Logan followed suit. They rode slowly, guns ready, towards the whitewashed walls of the old Mission. The Pima Indians paid them scant attention as they rode up.

In front of the Mission the white-haired Padre Juan was surrounded by squaws in bright-coloured dresses, and children of all sizes and ages, mostly naked. Beside Padre Juan stood Mona Durand in the dark green riding outfit.

Padre Juan lifted an arm in welcome as Jeb and Bob rode up and the squaws and children opened a reluctant lane for the riders. There was a worried look on the priest's weathered face.

"The runners have brought word," Padre Juan told the two riders, "of an Apache war party moving towards Picacho Pass on the Butterfield Overland Stage road. The Apaches number about fifty."

"Captain Logan of Quantrill's Confederate Cavalry," Mona Durand addressed Jeb in a mocking tone, the sunlight on her red hair, her lips parted in a faint smile. "The sun has not yet reached high noon. Two hours from now the stage coach will be entering Picacho Pass with a lone woman passenger. It's a forty-mile ride as the crow flies, further by trail." Mona spoke without panic or emotion and there was no way of reading what lay behind those grey-green eyes. "I thought you might like to know," she added.

Jeb sat his horse in silence. There was a whiteness to the set of his tight lips, a bleak look in his eyes as he listened to this girl calmly predict the Apache attack on the stage coach. He knew without being told that Mona was aware of where he had spent the night.

In the moment of silence that followed the dire tragic

38

prophecy, Jeb hated the girl. His lips thinned behind set teeth lest he speak his hatred. He had to tear his gaze away from her to look at Bob Leatherwood.

There was a grim hardened look on Bob's face that Jeb had seen on the bearded faces of Quantrill's men when they went into battle. A look that drove all humour from the little rebel's eyes, to leave them cold and merciless.

"Let's go, Jeb," he said in a strange voice that matched his eyes. He told Mona Durand to leave at once for Camp Lowell and tell the commanding officer to get his soldiers to the Pass as quickly as possible. The two men rode away.

Forty miles as the crow flies, she had said. Inwardly cursing the rough terrain ahead as Leatherwood took advantage of every short cut, they rode in silence at a long high trot that ate up the miles. Sometimes the trail narrowed, often there was no trail at all and the going was straight down, sliding the rumps of the horses. When Picacho· Peak loomed up in the distance, Bob pointed to it as he stood in his stirrups.

"Captain Hunter's Confederate Cavalry whipped the hell out of the damn yankee Californians in Picacho Pass," he said in a flat voice that held no note of triumph. "The Apaches wiped out a couple of Solomon Warner's freight outfits there. Set fire to the wagons, scalped the freighters and killed the mules. The Apaches travel on foot rather than horseback. They like horse meat and would butcher the finest animal ever foaled to make jerky." His words were flung back over his shoulder as he rode in the lead.

As the trail widened he slowed to a running walk to let his blowing horse get its second wind.

"It's time," he said, his voice waspish, "they sent cavalry to Camp Lowell instead of infantry. Lawdy man, when Cap Hunter was in Tucson the Confederates had saddle callouses an inch thick under the seat of their britches. He had the fear in them Apaches. Hunter's men had Apache scalps hanging like long fringe on the browbands of their bridles to keep the gnats and flies from their horses' eyes.

"Even by forced march it will be tomorrow afternoon before those Camp Lowell foot soldiers get to Picacho

39

Pass. By then there'll only be the red-headed turkey buzzards to fight off."

"What about the town citizens?" Jeb asked.

"They'll stay to defend the town, Jeb. With a liquor bottle in one hand and a gun in the other. Pete Kitchen and a few Injun fighters will saddle up and get there, but we'll all be too late."

"Looks like the stage line would furnish armed escort with Apaches on the prowl," Jeb said bitterly.

"A man would reckon so. Even if Durand didn't give a damn for the safety of his passengers and driver, those six-horse teams of his are the best horses that money can buy and a Concord coach runs into real dough. Maybe Matt carries insurance and don't give a damn."

"You make Durand sound cold-blooded as a snake."

"That's right, Jeb. Any man who would sell his only daughter to a thing like Major Sherwood would stoop to anything." There was contempt in Bob's voice as he took a flask from his pocket and drank. "That fancy Sherwood don't know what he's bargained for. Lawdy man, a shiver ran along my spine back yonder when she was talkin'. She's a flint off the Matt Durand block for sure." Leatherwood wiped the back of his glove across his mouth, and added, "I'd like to know how come Mona Durand got hold of Tondro's scalping knife."

"Maybe he's holed up at Durand's house," Jeb suggested.

"Could be, Jeb. Could be you got somethin' there."

"What's this Tondro look like?" asked Jeb.

"Never laid eyes on him. Few men around here have. They say he's tall, almost seven feet tall. A handsome bastard with the black eyes and long hair of an Injun. A half-breed Cherokee, so the story goes."

A white moon was pushing up over the broken skyline as they neared Picacho Peak. The high lone peak with its sheer cliffs and deep-cut narrow canyons stood like a giant monument in the desert wasteland. In the pale moonlight the black clefts between the grey walls, streaked white in places with the countless years of accumulated guano below the bat roosts, looked forbidding.

Picacho Peak was one of the landmarks shown on the maps of the Spanish Conquistadores. Buckskin scouts like

40

Pauline Weaver used it as a guide. General Fremont had seen it. Desert-rat prospectors had watched it through red-rimmed eyes as they crossed the parched land seeking gold.

Jeb Logan and Bob Leatherwood, following the stage road, passed it on the right as they rode cautiously, eyes peering ahead. The two men kept a grim silence, their guns ready, every nerve and muscle taut as they neared the pass.

That which they had ridden forty-odd miles to find, carrying the dread with them every foot of the long trail, lay directly ahead now, bathed in the ghostly white light of a winter moon.

The partly burned stage coach lay on its side, a little way off the rutted road, overturned by the runaway horses that had gotten out of control when the stage driver, mortally wounded, had dropped the lines. The lead team had turned too sharply, the swing team and the wheelers jackknifing in a tangle of chain traces and lead bars. A snapped-off wagon tongue, splintered double tree still held in place by the king pin, the broken spokes of the front wheel, all told the grim story.

The heavy leather boot in front under the driver's seat sagged empty, the mail sacks and pouches dragged out and cut open and plundered, the letters scattered and trampled in the dirt.

One of the lead team had been killed to stop the others. The horse had been skinned and the carcass carried away.

The stage driver and rifle guard had been dragged a short distance away. Both men had been scalped, their ears sliced off and bodies mutilated by Apache scalping knives.

The two riders found the body of the girl half way up the rocky, brush-choked slope. Her body had been muti-lated and her long, beautiful yellow hair was gone.

Jeb swung from his saddle. He pried the girl's fingers from their death grip around a square nickel-plated belt buckle with a few inches of soft glove leather attached. Jeb needed no second look to identify it as the buckle from the money belt he had given the girl. His hand trembled as he put the buckle in his pocket.

"Take care of her, Bob," Jeb said with emotion. "Stay

41

here till the soldiers show up. They'll have a rig of some kind to take the body back. I'd like to ride back alone."

"I understand, Jeb."

As Jeb rode away into the night he heard Bob Leatherwood hailing a score of horsebackers. Among them he heard the unmistakeable voice of Pete Kitchen.

A man with Jeb's guerrilla training, once he travelled a trail, could go back over it on the darkest night ever made. It was second nature. He uncorked the bottle he had in his pocket and took a big drink. The liquor burned in his empty belly and the warm glow made him a little giddy. As Leatherwood had predicted, the fever from the raw welts on his back was commencing to work. Jeb had been wounded twice while he followed Quantrill and he knew what lay in store for him, the throbbing pain, the fever, the nausea that went with it. A few hours from now he would need all the toughness he had to make the forty-mile ride over rough terrain to the Mission and the promised sanctuary of Padre Juan. He let his horse on loose rein, knowing the animal would take him there without guidance.

He had to grip the saddle horn with both hands to keep from falling off as he fought the dizzy spells. The blood had long since soaked through the bandages and seeped into his flannel shirt and dried there. Once or twice he thought he could hear the sound of shod hoofs behind him, but he figured if anyone was trailing him it would be Bob Leatherwood. It was in the little rebel's nature to follow, to make certain Jeb reached the Mission safely.

Jeb kept his gaze ahead watching for an Apache ambush as he rode in the black night. The darkness was all around him, but somehow he knew that the sky above was clear, filled with stars and a white moon riding high. Sheer instinct was keeping him balanced in the saddle, and when Pete Kitchen rode up alongside Jeb's horse that had stopped, Jeb was unaware of it.

It was sunrise when Pete Kitchen rode up to the Mission, leading the dun horse with Jeb tied in the saddle. "I got a sick feller, Padre Juan," Pete said, as he swung from his horse, jerking loose the ropes that tied Jeb in the saddle.

Pete Kitchen helped the priest get Jeb to the ground,

then he asked, "Where did you get hold of that big blue army mule I just saw in the pasture, Padre Juan?"

"A gift," answered the priest. "A gift from a Negro I buried one morning at sunrise."

Pete Kitchen carried Jeb into the adobe house Padre Juan reserved for his guests. "If this man dies," Pete told the priest, "Major Sherwood will be his murderer. Sherwood lacked the guts to fight a duel on account of a woman and had Logan strung up by the thumbs and given a lashing at the whippin' post. Wait till you see his back."

They sat Jeb on the edge of the bunk. The padre held him upright while Kitchen took off his boots and britches and the blood-soaked shirt. Then they laid him on his belly while the padre cut the crusted bandages off.

Pete Kitchen put Jeb's cartridge belt with the holstered guns on the table. He looked at the Bowie knife that he had taken from Jeb's scabbard. In that long moment while he examined the knife, thumbing the notches cut on the stag-horn handle, the steel grey eyes changed colour and took on the metallic glitter of the whetted blade in his hand. He slid his own Bowie knife from its sheath and shoved Tondro's into its place, then put his knife into Jeb's sheath and laid it on the table. The cold puzzled look still frosted his eyes when he spoke to the padre, whose back was towards him.

"I'll tend to the horses, Padre Juan. I'm better at that than nursin'."

"What about the Apaches at the Pass? asked Padre Juan.

"No more than a dozen of the murderin' sons of hell," Pete spat disgustedly. "Scattered like quail when they burned the stage. Killed the two men and the girl, scalpin' 'em all. If these Pima Injuns of yours had the guts of a cottontail, they could tromp those Apaches to death. You baby these gut eaters, Padre. Psalm singin' don't mix with fightin'." Pete chuckled, the hard eyes puckered. It was an argument that came up whenever the brown-frocked priest and the hardened Indian fighter met.

"While we don't see exactly eye to eye on some things, Padre," said Pete Kitchen, "we savvy one another. You know how to keep your silence. This wounded man under your roof is a wanted man, marked for death. Jeb Logan is a Quantrill Guerrilla with a price on his head and he's had a run-in with Major Sherwood."

Padre Juan straightened his back, a pair of surgical scissors in one hand, the bunched blood-caked bandages in the other. There was a grimness to his seamed, weathered face. A shadow darkened his warm brown eyes. Eyes that had looked into the hearts and souls of too many sinners.

"What are you tryin' to tell me, Pete?" he asked quietly.

"This, my good friend. If ever that yankee Major Sherwood or Matt Durand get word that Captain Jeb Logan is under your roof, a bunch of blue coat soldiers will show up with fixed bayonets and demand that you turn the sick man over to them. Your SANCTUARY sign over the doorway won't stop them," Pete told the priest.

Padre Juan smiled and said, "They will be forced to run their bayonets through me before they enter the door. They will hesitate before they violate God's humble dwelling."

"You win, Padre." Pete smiled. "Like you always win." His hand slapped the butt of the big Colt gun along his thigh. "I am handier with this than I am with words," he added, backing through the door.

Padre Juan closed the door. He dippered some clear cool water in a gourd from the red clay-baked olla that hung in a rawhide sling from the ridge log, and held the water to Jeb's parched lips.

Jeb twisted his head on the pillow, clarity in his pain-seared eyes. "I heard what was said, Padre Juan. The man was Pete Kitchen."

"Perhaps you owe your life to Pete Kitchen. He tied you on your saddle and fetched you here."

"That makes me beholden to the man who killed . . ." Jeb bit the accusation off. "To a man I don't trust," he finished lamely.

"Pete Kitchen's faults are many, his virtues few," said the priest. "I also am beholden to the man who has befriended me and this Mission with his life." Padre Juan's words were a gentle rebuke.

"I am an ungrateful guest, Padre Juan. Forgive me."

"You are sick. There is nothing to forgive." The priest

44

hung the empty gourd by a rawhide thong to a wooden peg driven into the three-foot adobe wall. He brought back a bottle of brandy and two glasses from the shelf. "Fortification against the pain, Señor Jeb. I am going to bathe those raw welts with a carbolic solution that will hurt like the liquid fire of hell." Sparks showed in the brown eyes. "Then I'll use some horse salve from the saddle bag belonging to your little rebel companion that he sent along with Pete Kitchen. I trust no harm befell the little man. I have a fondness for him and his fiery rebel speeches."

"He is fine, Padre. I told him to stay with the dead girl."

"I think he advised Pete Kitchen to follow you, knowing you were in no fit condition to make the long horseback ride back alone." He held the brandy to Jeb's mouth, then started sponging the raw welts with the carbolic solution.

Outside, Pete Kitchen cared for both horses, sponging the sweaty backs as they ate split corn from the canvas morral strapped over each horse's head. He went to the pasture to catch a fresh horse he had left there for his use whenever he needed a change of mounts, and again noticed the blue mule that had belonged to the Negro. He walked slowly around the animal, examining it from all sides. It wore no government brand, either Union or Confederate. If Pete Kitchen was any judge of mules, and he was, this one's dam must have been a thoroughbred mare and the Jack that sired the mule was of the same fine breeding. When Pete had sized the mule up and recognized it as a fine animal, he looked into its mouth to judge the age.

He was saddling his own horse, when he saw Mona Durand top the rise on her bay horse. His wide mouth spread in a grin that showed his big white teeth. Pete had an excellent eye for a good horse or mule, or a handsome woman or a pretty girl. He had his hat in his hand when Mona rode up.

"I came here to find Captain Jeb Logan, Mr. Kitchen," Mona spoke cautiously. "Perhaps you can tell me where to look for him."

"Perhaps." Pete Kitchen put on his hat, his eyes cold

and wary as the girl's. "On the other hand, perhaps not. It all depends, Miss Mona Durand."

"Whether I'm here on my own," she said, her tone faintly mocking, "or as a spy for the brave Major Sherwood and my father?"

"You hit the bullseye, lady."

"I'm here on my own behalf. I'm the cause of that disgraceful deal Jeb Logan got at the whipping post, and for something else that happened here at the Mission." She pointed her riding crop at the gaunt-flanked dun horse under the thatched roofed ramada. "That's Jeb Logan's dun horse," she said.

"Step down and rest your saddle, lady. Stay here. I'll be back directly I locate Padre Juan," Pete Kitchen told her, walking towards the cabin where Jeb was.

Padre Juan opened the door and stepped outside, shutting the door quickly as the girl slid her horse to a halt and was on the ground beside the priest before Pete got there.

"If Jeb Logan is in there, Padre Juan," she said in a brittle voice, the blood drained from her face, "I'll crawl on my knees to beg his forgiveness. If he's dying, I'm to blame."

The padre's strong hands gripped her shoulders. He opened the door for her to enter, closing it gently behind her.

Pete Kitchen stood tracked, a faint smile on his mouth, his eyes puckered. "Por Dios, Padre, this thing builds up more dangerous by the hour. Better wake Jeb Logan up and fill his two hands with guns. I'll ride picket and give the rebel yell when the damn yankees top the rise."

"Señor Jeb is awake," said the priest. "Let us partake of some breakfast, Compadre Pete." His arms folded, hands tucked into the sleeves of his robe, he led the way.

"I wish to hell," Pete Kitchen said, his hand sliding along his holstered gun, "that Bob Leatherwood would ride up to take the deal. Hell's fire, I'm no rebel. You'll excuse the cussin', Padre Juan, but we're all in a hell of a mess." Kitchen's boisterous laugh battered the quiet.

Jeb Logan heard the faint echo of the laugh but paid it no heed. All his attention was centered on the girl. The pain and torture of the long ride, the padre's dressing of his wounds had left him exhausted, and now that the glass of brandy was taking effect, a hazy relaxation was setting in. His squinted eyes were a little out of focus, the clearness blurred as he looked at Mona Durand, not believing what he saw.

She wore an Indian-tanned buckskin shirt to match the divided skirt that came below the knees and over the top of her custom-made cavalry boots. A man's grey stetson hat was pulled down to cover her heavy copper-red hair that was plaited in two thick squaw braids and coiled at the nape of her neck. A large black silk neck handkerchief was knotted loosely around her throat, a red sash tied around her slim waist. Her lips were parted in an uncertain smile as the grey-green eyes looked at him, her back against the thick slab door of the cabin. The girl went rigid as Pete Kitchen's loud laugh echoed inside the adobe walls.

"Pete Kitchen," Mona Durand said. "I don't trust that man." She slid the heavy wooden bar in place to lock the door and came slowly across the hard-packed dirt floor to stand alongside the bunk.

Jeb lay on his side facing her. He wore a clean white nightshirt the padre had put on him. A light wool blanket covered him.

"I'm the cause," Mona said, looking down at him, "of all your suffering, Jeb Logan. I am truly sorry for the brutal words I spoke. It was cowardly and mean. I'm glad I have this chance to tell you what kind of a person I am: spoiled, selfish, vindictive, hateful and spiteful."

Mona stopped talking and picked up the leather-sheathed Bowie knife, a strange bright glitter in her eyes that changed them to hard emerald green. "Is this the knife I used to cut you free?" she asked.

"Yes," Jeb answered. He did not know that Pete Kitchen had switched knives.

"I'm taking it back with me," she said. "I came here to beg your forgiveness, also to warn you. As soon as you are in shape to ride a horse, quit this godforsaken country before they hunt you down like a vicious animal and kill or hang you." She held the sheathed knife in her hand and added, "This knife has something to do with it. There

47

was a terrific commotion when it turned up missing. You'd think some thief had stolen the crown jewels."

"Where did you get the knife?" Jeb spoke for the first time.

"In our kitchen. Somebody had used it to slice off some meat from a cold roast of venison on the kitchen table. I grabbed it as I ran out the kitchen door to get my horse." She shoved the knife into the red sash around her waist, covering the handle with a fold of the silk.

"I'd better be getting back to Tucson," she said, "before I'm missed and trailed here. Promise me you'll quit the country, Jeb Logan." She took one of his hands in both hers. Her hands felt cold.

"I can't promise that. I came here for a purpose. I won't leave till I accomplish what I came here to do," Jeb's eyes were bleak.

"You rode to Picacho Peak," her hands gripped tight. "Did you . . . ?"

"Yes. The girl's body had been mutilated and she'd been scalped."

"Fay Wayne was Major Sherwood's mistress," Mona said quietly. "I'll see that she gets a decent burial." She released her hands and held his face with the black stubble. Her lips were warmly soft against his mouth and a dry sob came from her tight throat.

A sharp rapping on the door broke them apart.

"Time to go," the voice of Padre Juan came through the door. "Pete Kitchen has sighted a small detachment of cavalry approaching."

Mona Durand slid the bar back and opened the door. The priest handed her the bridle reins and she mounted and was gone in a cloud of heavy dust.

Jeb Logan threw back the blanket, swinging his bare legs over the edge of the bunk. He had a long-barrelled Colt gun in each hand when the padre came in. Jeb laid the two guns on the bunk and reached for his pants and boots, putting them on.

"Bar the door when I leave, Jeb," said Padre Juan. "I've made a small wager with Pete Kitchen, to end the argument between us that the cross is mightier than the sword. If I lose the wager, then you can use your pistols.

Is that agreed?" There was a twinkle in the warm brown eyes.

"Agreed, Padre Juan. I have brought you nothing but trouble."

"Oftentimes trouble is a blessing in disguise," the priest said, closing the door as he went out. Jeb crossed the room and slid the wooden bar in place. The old bell in the Mission commenced ringing.

The odor of food from the white-covered tray the priest had brought in assailed his nostrils. For the first time Jeb felt hunger gnawing at his empty belly. He tucked the tails of his nightshirt into the waistband of his pants and sat on the edge of the bed with the tray that held a huge platter of home-cured, broiled ham and a large mound of fried potatoes, dutch-oven sourdough biscuits, thick gravy, and a large pot of black coffee. Jeb wolfed his food, washing it down with the hot coffee, and was wiping up the last of the gravy with biscuits when he heard an army officer giving commands to his men.

"Company halt! At ease!" And in a more quiet voice that held the hint of an Irish brogue, he called out, "Merry Christmas, Padre! If the orders had come at an earlier hour, I would have been in time to kneel with the converted heathens at six o'clock mass. I have orders to carry out an unpleasant duty, Padre Juan."

"What is this unpleasant duty, Captain Slattery?"

"Word was received at Camp Lowell that you are harbouring a wanted man, a Captain Jeb Logan, a Quantrill Guerrilla. I have orders to bring him in."

Padre Juan said, his voice deep-toned, "Heed the sign above the door of my humble dwelling, Captain."

"SANCTUARY!" Captain Slattery read aloud. He repeated the word, then clearing his throat, he used his best parade voice: "Sergeant, take the men back to Tucson. I'll overtake you before you get there. Company dismissed!"

Inside the cabin Jeb shoved the guns into their holsters. Padre Juan had won his wager, hands down and by the faith of the Irish.

The adobe house, built a half century ago was provided with gun ports and peep holes. Jeb watched the priest hand the bridle reins to an Indian to take care of the

Captain's horse, then led the tall young Irishman into the patio and his quarters behind the Mission. They were inside when Pete Kitchen, leading the bay horse with Mona Durand in the saddle, rode into sight. Pete lifted his voice to a loud hello and the priest and the Captain came out.

"I want you to give this young lady armed escort to Tucson, Captain," Kitchen said to Slattery. "It's not healthy for a lone white woman to be riding around, with an Apache war party on the prowl. See that she don't give you the slip. I warn you Mona Durand fights like a wild cat."

Pete handed the girl's bridle reins to the Captain, who looked embarrassed. As Kitchen rode away, Jeb saw him pull up alongside the blue mule that was in the pasture. For the second time that morning the Indian fighter looked the mule over from all angles, taking his time. An uneasy look crept into Jeb's eyes. Bugler Stack had ridden the mule while he accompanied Jeb's father, the one-armed Colonel Wentworth, on his mission through this part of the country.

"That man you came here to put under arrest, Captain Slattery, Jeb Logan, the Confederate," Jeb heard Mona Durand ask. "What will you do about him?"

"I respect the sign over the padre's doorway," answered Slattery. "No man could do otherwise and hold his head up as an officer and a gentleman." The smile was gone from his sunburned face, leaving his eyes cold blue. "Regardless of Major Sherwood's orders."

"It will be a pleasure to ride back with you, Captain Slattery." Mona's voice had a tightness to it.

Jeb Logan watched them ride out of sight. He sat on the edge of the bunk staring into space, a brooding look in his eyes. Padre Juan found him like that when he came in, and said, "You have need of twenty-four hours rest, Señor Jeb. You'll be safe here until you are in shape to travel. Pete Kitchen is on the trail of the Apache war party."

"You won your wager," Jeb said as the priest helped him off with his boots. "What was the nature of it?"

"That Pete Kitchen accompany his wife to high mass on Easter Sunday."

"And if you lost the wager, Padre?"

50

"He wanted me to wager the blue mule, but I refused on the grounds that it was a gift. We settled the wager for a jug of brandy."

"You told him about the Negro?" Jeb inquired, a worried expression in his eyes.

"Only that the mule was a gift left by a Negro I buried. No more than that. Have I revealed too much, Señor?"

"No. It is nothing that matters."

Jeb lay down on his belly to relieve the pain that seared his back like a slab of hot metal. He twisted his head on the pillow to ask a question. "Have you any maps, Padre Juan, that show the location of the old Spanish Land Grants?"

"There are several, dating back to the map made by Padre Kino, and no man was better qualified to mark the boundary lines than that Jesuit, whom the Indians called the Black Robe. He was a horseman to excel all men on horseback or on the back of a mule. His long rides were prodigious, setting a record for time and distance never equalled. The map he carefully drew and measured in leagues I consider accurate.

"There are other maps dated at the time of the Gadsden Purchase. The greed of mankind is on the later maps and the quill should have been dipped in human blood to mark these later controversial boundary lines." The padre's voice was vibrant, his warm eyes shadowed.

"I am well aware of the blood of which you speak, Padre Juan. Mine is no idle curiosity."

"When you have rested, we shall go over the maps together." He laid a hand on Jeb's shoulder. "Try to sleep now," he said kindly.

When Padre Juan had gone Jeb got up and barred the door, then lay down on the bunk, his two guns within easy reach. He closed his eyes tightly as he tried to puzzle things out, fit each part into the whole pattern of things.

It was best to go back to the letter from his father that Bugler Stack had brought him and was in the money belt he had given the girl. The letter had told of his father's secret and dangerous mission into a hostile land to bribe, cajole and as a last resort threaten the Mexican politicos and army leaders of Sonora, Mexico, to revolt or secede Sonora as a part of the Gadsden Purchase.

He had told how the Confederacy had given him the La Jornada Grant, dating back to the early Spanish conquistadores, a vast square solid block of land, each side seventy-five miles long. It was outlined on but one map made by Padre Kino, a Jesuit Priest.

Jeb was remembering his father's letter word for word. He wished he had the letter now because he knew if it were read it could mean his death warrant.

Tears squeezed from under his tight eyelids until finally he slept. It was the dead sleep of utter exhaustion, the brother of death.

6

It was almost twenty-four hours later when Padre Juan and Jeb Logan sat down at the table to look over Padre Kino's old map, the corners weighted down to hold the roll in place. Other rolled maps lay on the floor.

Jeb, rested, bathed and shaved, with the healing salve easing the pain of his lacerated back, his belly full, felt fit to travel.

Each hour's delay, every minute, increased his danger here. He was impatient to be on his way, but he gave no outward sign of it as he listened to the older man's every word, memorizing every detail of Padre Kino's map.

"Captain Francisco Vasquez de Coronado," Padre Juan sat back in his chair, his hands tucked into the loose sleeves of his robe, "on his vain search for the fabled Seven Cities of Cibola, in the year 1540, granted this land to one of his lieutenants. Coronado wanted the message of his failure to be taken ahead of his return to the City of Mexico, and this young Lieutenant Estebán de la Guerra volunteered to take the message. Coronado mounted him on his finest horse and the Lieutenant departed at daybreak.

" 'From this place to whatever point you reach at nightfall,' Captain de Coronado told Estebán de la Guerra, 'I grant you the land you cover in your first day's journey. The width of the land will be measured in the exact leagues you travel on the day's journey, and the entire square block shall be given to you, to remain in the name of your family for all time'."

Padre Juan smiled gently as he filled their empty glasses before he continued with the story.

"Estebán de la Guerra was an excellent horseman and he knew how to get the utmost in miles from the horse under him. He had covered many leagues when he camped at nightfall. In miles, about seventy-five. He piled rocks along the roadside for a monument to mark the place. When he had cared for his horse and eaten a frugal meal, he lay down to rest his weary bones. That night he was attacked by Indians and killed, for he was travelling alone in hostile country.

"Captain de Coronado, travelling the El Camino Real many days later, found his dead body beside the pile of rocks. He buried the lieutenant there. Fashioning a cross out of his broken sword that lay in the dust, he placed it in the rock monument. Then he marked the square of land on the map he carried with him.

"When Coronado, broken by his failure to find the Seven Cities of Cibola, returned to the City of Mexico with the news of his defeat, he was a disgraced and unhappy man, but he kept his word and recorded the land grant in the name of Estebán de la Guerra and his true heirs, according to his agreement. He named the grant *La Jornada*, meaning a day's journey on horseback. A century later Padre Kino marked it on his map, because Kino was a faithful and painstaking historian."

Jeb Logan had been sitting straddle of a bench while he listened to the priest's long story. "You are entitled to know," Jeb finally spoke, "why I am so vitally interested in La Jornada, Padre Juan."

"I am possessed by a man's natural curiosity," the priest said quietly. "At the same time I sense your reluctance to talk, so let matters stand as they are."

"It is a dangerous thing to know, Padre," Jeb said, measuring his words. "But when the danger is no longer present, I promise to share the secret I carry with me now." Jeb got to his feet and the two men touched glasses and drank.

Jeb saddled the dun horse. Dusk had thickened into darkness as he mounted. He thanked the priest for the sanctuary of his house, for the food and drink. He promised to return.

"*Vaya con Dios!*" Padre Juan lifted his arm, making the sign of the cross in the starlight as he watched horse and rider until they were swallowed in the night. The Mission bell rang out the summons for evening vespers and the priest walked slowly with bent head, the shadow of sorrow in his eyes for the man who was riding alone into danger.

El Camino Real was worn by countless men such as Jeb Logan. Men with the call of high adventure in their hearts, the light of it showing in their eyes. Other men, less courageous, avoiding the open road to skulk in the shadows, craven, cowardly men of all races, who preyed on the reckless and brave, setting deadly ambushes along the road.

Vaya con Dios! God protect you! Jeb Logan had need of that protection, but for the nearness of his hands to the two Colt guns, he gave no sign of it. There had been no further word of danger from Tucson. Bob Leatherwood had sent no warning message. Pete Kitchen was trailing Apaches. No more soldiers had come near the Mission and Mona Durand had paid him no further visit.

The night air was crisp, without trace of wind. Perhaps there would be a coating of frost on the grass by morning. The mountains were outlined against the star-filled sky. The dun horse was grained and fresh between his legs. Padre Juan had stuffed his saddle bags.

El Camino Real followed the Santa Cruz river the length of the wide valley. Taking the line of least resistance, the road twisted in lazy, careless fashion through giant old cottonwood trees that offered protective shade from the merciless daytime sun. The big trees were bare limbed now, skeleton frames against the moonless sky as Jeb Logan let his horse choose its own gait. He passed the mud huts of small Pima villages with the underbrush cleared, planted in maize and chili during the warmer months, but barren ground now, the *acequias* choked with dry weeds. No light showed from the huts that were made of saguaro and ocotillo ribs and adobe mud. No campfire burned. No sign of human life, not even the cry of a hungry or sick baby squawling for breast feeding. Even the mongrel dogs that skulked through the brush on the prowl for rabbits did not bark. But Jeb knew that more than a few pairs of beady black eyes viewed his passing and that before he reached a bend in the road a quarter mile away, the whispered warning of the white man's coming would precede him.

To Jeb Logan this was a strange country and he was unused to friendly Indians. He and the Negro had come through hostile land, and it gave him an uneasy feeling to be watched. He was a white man riding alone at night, at the mercy of an enemy.

Just when and how he became aware of the fact that he was being followed, he did not know. It was the way his horse travelled, the moving of the black ears, the slight turning of the dun's head and the unevenness of the running walk that he first noticed. The horse was acting as though there were other horses behind, and horses meant riders. Jeb felt a sort of prickling along his scalp as he slid one of his guns from the holster and rode with it between his lean belly and the fork of his saddle. When he sighted a thick clump of mesquite brush ahead he rode past it, quitting the road to ride in behind it, reining up in the black shadows, a gun in each hand.

The years with Quantrill's Guerrillas had schooled Jeb in every trick and countermove there was to be learned in bushwhacker fighting—the dodging and hiding, the shooting and running. Quantrill was a pastmaster at guerrilla warfare, his handful of hard riding followers pitted against overwhelming forces. Jeb had learned at the beginning that it was every man for himself.

Somehow Jeb knew, even before they rode into sight, that they would be white men, who would be either drunk or slovenly careless, ignorant in the cunning and craft of the trail, because a man trained to follow a trail or elude pursuers, would have taken every precaution to remain undiscovered until the gun trap was sprung.

Before the two horsebackers rode into sight in the dim starlight, the sound of their voices, the jingle of bit chains, the creak of new saddle leather, overrode the dulled thud of shod hoofs on the rutted, dusty road.

"Slow down, Sarge." The voice had a thick blur, as if the speaker, mouthing his words over a quid of soggy tobacco in his cheek, was a little drunk. "That crazy bastard Logan might be bushed up ahead. I don't want to die so young."

"The sooner we overtake that rebel and fill him full of

lead, the quicker we get the bounty money to spend."
The second voice had a saw-edge that Jeb recognized as
belonging to Sergeant Burch, the man who had put the
raw welts on his back. "Take a drink to wash the yellow
that's crawled into your neck, Smithson. Shoot that Quantrill outlaw if he shows. Major Sherwood said we could
write our own ticket if we got him."

Jeb Logan jumped his horse from the brush to block
the road. He had a gun in each hand. "The sooner the
quicker," Jeb's voice was flat. "Let's have at it, you two
bounty hunters."

He recognized the lanky, lantern-jawed Smithson as the
one who had strung him up by the thumbs.

"Don't shoot!" Smithson's arms lifted high. "I'm just a
buck private followin' orders. I didn't want to come."

"Shut up," said Jeb. "Unbuckle that belt and drop it.
Make a move to lift that holster flap and you'll get a .44
slug in your brisket."

Jeb's eyes were slivered as he looked at the beefy sergeant, whose face bore the scars of Mona Durand's riding
crop. "That goes double for you, loud mouth. I hope you
make a gun move."

Both soldiers unbuckled their gun belts and let them
fall in the dust.

"Dismount. Unsaddle and turn loose," ordered Jeb. "If
your luck holds out, you'll go back on foot to Camp
Lowell." Jeb's teeth bared in wolfish grin.

When the two men had turned their horses loose and
stood with their hands lifted, Jeb unbuckled his rope
strap and threw his rawhide reata over the bare limb of a
cottonwood. He told Smithson to put the noose around the
sergeant's wrists, and as the noose tightened Jeb took his
turns around the saddle horn and dragged the beefy man
until both feet were off the ground, the toes barely touching dirt, then fastened the reata around the tree trunk.

Jeb dismounted and told Smithson to lie flat on his belly
with his hands behind him. He tied the man's wrists together. Taking out his jackknife, he cut away the sergeant's
coat and shirt. Then taking his braided rawhide quirt
from the saddle horn he swung it across the man's bare
back. Jeb gave him a half dozen lashes and when the man
kept begging and yelping with pain, he slashed the quirt

57

across the slack-jawed mouth. Sickening of the brutal job, Jeb slacked the reata. Sergeant Burch fell to the ground in a shapeless heap.

Jeb fastened the reata to the other man's wrists and strung him up despite the soldier's drunken begging and sobbing. He gave him the same punishment before slackening the rope and letting him fall beside his companion.

Jeb coiled the reata and buckled it on his saddle and hung the quirt on the horn. He picked up the two webbed belts and removed the two guns from their army holsters and fastened the guns to his cartridge belt. Then he mounted and rode away, leaving the two soldiers where they had fallen.

Jeb was aware that he had been watched as he wielded the quirt, and felt sure it was one of the Pimas who shifted his position behind the brush to get a better view of the white man's punishment of two men of his own race. By sunrise the news would reach the ears of Padre Juan at the Mission.

As Jeb wiped the sweat from his face with an unsteady hand, his only regret for the brutal punishment he had meted out to the pair of soldiers, was that the priest would hear about it—that and the fact that he had wasted too much time.

The lopsided white moon was riding high when he left there. He uncorked the bottle of brandy the padre had put in his saddle bag and drank as a thirsty man drinks water. The exertion had brought the sweat out and his own back was a mass of hellish itching, throbbing pain. He wanted to rub his back against the trunk of a tree to relieve the itching, but he fought off the urge, and rode on at a jog trot.

It was nearing daybreak when he turned off El Camino Real, to ride into the dark shadows of Madera Canyon. In the pale light of the false dawn that preceded the sunrise, he located the landmarks the Negro had described for him time and again. There in the silence with the pale light fading the stars, Jeb found the grave of his father where the Negro had etched a deep X with a knife in a granite boulder.

Jeb stood there for a while, his hat in his hand, his head bowed as if in prayer. His grief was deep-rooted. Too many memories were haunting him like unseen ghosts in the hushed silence of the canyon. An aching lump had come into his throat as he conjured up the picture of his father: a tall, spare man with iron grey hair and moustache and goatee; a handsome lean-jawed man, with smoke grey eyes under heavy brows; a stern man with the straight back of the military. He had been too stern, perhaps, for a father's understanding of a son who had been headstrong in his colt's stride. Wentworth Logan had been exacting in the bringing up of a motherless boy. A true Kentuckian and a gentleman of the South, his ideals of womanhood placed on a high pedestal, and those fine principles he had passed on to Jeb.

Standing there in the early dawn at the grave, Jeb knew inside his heart that his father had never wholly forgiven him for the black disgrace he had brought on an honoured name by joining Quantrill's Guerrillas.

In the grave was the large brass telescope with the rolled parchment title to the La Jornada Land Grant, which was his for the claiming, to hold against the overwhelming strength of the Union Government.

Granted that Colonel Wentworth Logan had died in the strong belief of Confederate victory, even if the Confederate States of the South had won the Civil War, the La Jornada Land Grant was a border wasteland with the smouldering hatred of the Mexicans for the gringos of the north; an untamed country, swarming with Apache Indians. Wentworth Logan had bequeathed his only son something that would mould him into true manhood, or kill him.

A hard, bitter grin spread Jeb's tight-lipped mouth. He would abide by the last wishes of his father, who had lived and died true to his stern code of honour. Jeb was almost grateful for it. A man is measured by his own standards. So be it. Jeb Logan would live and die according to his own code, according to his own lights.

Let the map and the parchment stay rolled in the old brass telescope. When he had avenged his father's murder he would come back here, decide then if it was worth while digging up a thing that had no value in the eyes of the Union Government.

Jeb held no bitterness against the last dictates of his

father. The dead man had left a challenge for him to take up. In that moment as he stood there, head lifted, Jeb knew and understood his father for the first time. He wished he could tell him that he accepted the challenge; that he wanted it no other way.

Jeb mounted and rode into the early dawn. Streaks of red slashed like knife wounds across a sky that was the dull colour of cartridge lead. He was headed for Pete Kitchen's ranch on Potrero Creek near Calabazas, a few miles north of the Mexican border, a day's easy ride for horse and man.

7

THE DAY had begun with a red-streaked sunrise. It was ending now in a vivid, blood-splashed sky that seeped through the desert haze along the mountains.

Jeb Logan had timed his arrival at Pete Kitchen's El Potrero Rancho for the supper hour when the man was most apt to be home.

Smoke spiraled skyward from the chimney of the house on top of the hill. Cattle were scattered, grazing along the creek. One of his Mexican vaqueros rode into sight, headed for the home ranch and a warm supper after a long day's ride. He was singing an old ranchero song as his horse followed the trail.

The song broke off abruptly. There was a short moment of blank silence. Then the shrill scream knifed the peaceful quiet. The vaquero swayed, grabbing the saddle horn for balance as his spurs dug deep and the running horse headed up the slope of the hill. The blood-curdling war cry of the Apaches drowned out the thin scream of the wounded Mexican, the feathered tip of an arrow between shoulder blades, as he slumped across the neck of his horse. The sharp crack of a rifle came from the lookout on the walk-way on top of the house. Somewhere from inside the house a woman's scream needled through and was lost in the yelling of the Apaches who sprang from behind every bush and boulder. The Indians had surrounded the hill and were now running, half crouched, zigzagging, in an upward circle that narrowed with the slope of the hill. A second gun from the walk-way was spewing fire from the top of the house.

The running horse reached the hilltop and ducked in under the thatched roof of a long ramada, throwing the

61

wounded rider. A woman and a girl ran out, dragging the vaquero inside and slamming the door shut.

Jeb Logan sat his horse behind a patch of heavy brush, holding back, his slivered eyes watching the naked, war-painted Apaches appear as if by magic from the bowels of hell. Yelling and screaming their blood chant, with bows and arrows, spears and knives in their hands, they tightened the circle and corkscrewed up the hill. Jeb's knotted bridle reins were dropped across his saddle horn. He held a gun in each hand, the two holstered guns in his belt shoved forward against his lean belly.

When the last Indian left the shelter of brush and rocks and joined the tightening circle, Jeb jumped the dun horse from the brush and headed straight for the circling redskins. His lips were skinned back from his teeth and standing high in his stirrups, his guns spewing death, he let out a rebel yell as he charged.

Years of pistol practice were paying off now. He was a dead shot with either hand. Both guns fired without aiming, the barrels pointed at the moving target and the trigger pulled. Each .44 slug hit its mark as the blazing guns blasted a wide gap in the Apache circle. When the guns were empty, he shoved them in their holsters and jerked the spare guns with a swift, unbroken movement. His knees moved the dun horse at a slant against the direction of the running Apaches, the guns cutting a swath of death.

A tall, sinewy Apache, paint and grease slicked, sprang up beside Jeb's horse, grabbing the bridle reins. He had a scalping knife in his hand, and tied to his grease matted black hair was a long eagle feather and a scalplock of yellow hair. Letting go the bridle reins the Apache grabbed Jeb's saddle horn, so close the spittle from his screaming mouth sprayed Jeb as the Indian swung upward with the momentum of the running horse. Another moment and the Apache would be straddle of the horse at Jeb's back.

Jeb shoved the barrel of his gun into the Indian's open mouth and pulled the trigger. The Apache's hand had somehow fouled in the quirt-loop on the saddle horn and the greased body now hung limp. Then the horse kicked him loose, ripping and tearing at the naked belly until the hand slipped free.

Jeb twisted his head around quickly to take a split-second look at the Apache sprawled on his back, the belly gone, the lower half of the body torn away and fifty feet behind. Then Jeb's two guns were once more blasting the warriors.

There was a new tone to the Apache war chant now. A dismal off-key wail that passed along the line of encircling Indians. The circle broke apart as they turned back down the slope, running for the shelter of brush and boulder from which they had sprung into being. The death chant filled the red dusk, the war shout gone. Savage grief had taken the fight out of their hearts.

Jeb Logan headed his winded horse up the slope of the hill. He could see a Mexican woman and a boy on the walkway on the roof as they lifted their heads and shoulders cautiously to take a look. Both had long-barrelled rifles gripped and ready. The woman called to him as he rode up. "Ride into the corral, Señor." Her voice was vibrant with emotion. "I will send Pedrito down to care for your horse. I am Doña Rosa, wife of Pete Kitchen." She spoke in a blending mixture of border American and Mexican. "Later I will express my gratitude."

"Por nada." Jeb pulled the hat from his sweat-matted head. He dismounted and opened the pole gate of the large mesquite corral that was a high stockade, to protect the small remuda of saddle horses and mules inside. There was a filled water trough and a long rack filled with hay. Jeb unsaddled. He was unaware of the boy's presence until he spoke.

"I have filled this *morral* as full as it will hold of cracked corn and barley, Señor," he said, handing Jeb the canvas bag to hang on the horse's head.

"I am Pedrito. Pete Kitchen is my patrón," the boy said proudly. "The Apaches killed my parents. *Por Dios,* Señor, never have I seen such a thing–two pistols shooting and your horse on a dead run. I forgot to shoot and was on my feet yelling for you when Doña Rosa pulled me down." The boy's eyes were hard and shining, bright with excitement. "Two pistols! *Dios hombre!*"

The colour was returning to Jeb's face. He looked at the boy closely. "How is the wounded vaquero?" he asked.

"Eduardo lives. The arrow went deep. The pain is in

63

his eyes and not on his tongue. Eduardo is concerned only for his wife who is having a baby."

Jeb reached for his saddle bag that held the medicine Bob Leatherwood had put there. The glint of steel caught his eye as he stooped over the saddle. The Apache's scalping knife was slanted into the high cantle of his saddle. The blade had gone through the leather and into the wood with a savage thrust that would have ripped Jeb wide open across his kidneys. The bleak look was back in his eyes as he stared at the rawhide wrapped handle, dark-stained with crusted dried blood. Jeb knew the dried blood on the knife belonged to Fay Wayne, and as his hand reached to pull it out, he drew back with a sudden jerk and let the knife stay.

With the saddle bag in his hand, Jeb headed for the house with quick strides, leaving the boy to close the corral gate.

A Mexican girl in her 'teens opened the door as he neared the house. The vaquero lay on his belly on the floor, the feathered arrow shaft showing. Pain seared his black eyes as he twisted his head to look at the man who stood over him. His blood crawled the scrubbed pine board floor.

Jeb took a half-emptied bottle of brandy from his saddle bag and holding the Mexican's head up, he held it to his mouth.

Jeb asked the girl to heat water and bring clean bandages, then with an unbroken slow pull, so as not to tear the flesh more than necessary, he removed the arrow. He cut away the vaquero's jacket and shirt. No groan, no whimper of pain came from behind the bared, clenched teeth of the wounded man, the black eyes squinted tightly shut.

Memory flashed through Jeb's thoughts to the arrow he had withdrawn from the Negro's flesh, the skin bluish-black with approaching death. Jeb pushed the memory back as he bathed the Mexican's wound and wadded cotton into the slit, covering it with strips of clean cloth.

"I am grateful, señor. There will be a prayer," the vaquero said and started crawling towards the bedroom where his wife was having her first baby.

Jeb climbed the ladder to the walk-way around the roof.

"You are needed below, Señora," he told the handsome, black haired, buxom wife of Pete Kitchen.

"God will reward you, Señor," Doña Rosa said quietly as she touched his hand, taking the rifle with her. She gestured towards three rifles and an open box of ammunition. "The guns are loaded," she explained and went down the ladder.

Jeb walked, crouched, along the narrow planks, a long-barrelled rifle in his hands. He could detect no movement in the brush and rocks below. The Apache death chant had died out, leaving a silence that was pregnant with danger as the shadows of night crept in. There was nothing to do but wait the long night with the chill of winter in the air.

Jeb stared out across the country towards the ragged mountains that showed black against the deep purple of sky, keeping his gaze fastened there for a time. The reaction was setting in as the man knew it would. He was not yet ready to look down the slope of the hill where the dead Apaches lay sprawled in awkward shapes.

Pedrito came up the ladder, a basket covered by a clean white dishcloth under one arm. It was filled with food and a bottle of mescal and a jug of water. Pedrito said, "Doña Rosa and my cousin Eduardo wish to know your name, Señor, so that the new born baby boy shall be named in your honour."

"Jeb," he said, the brooding hardness of his eyes melting. "Jeb Logan."

Pedrito slid down the ladder and out of sight, leaving Jeb with a twisted smile on his face. A Mexican baby, born during an Apache raid, named for him. Padre Juan would get the story when the baby was taken to the Mission for baptismal christening. Jeb pulled the corncob stopper of the bottle of mescal and lifted it in salutation of the new baby, the grin on his mouth a strange quirk. He was recalling the nature of the grim errand that had brought him to El Potrero.

When Pedrito came back up the ladder, Jeb took the cloth from the basket. There was a big bowl of chili beans and jerky that gave off a savory spiced odour. A plate filled with flour tortillas, and an earthenware pot of hot

65

black coffee. Never had hot food been more welcome, and Jeb said so.

The boy eyed the holstered guns. "How long did you have to practice to use two pistols with your horse at a run?" he asked.

"A long time, Pedrito," Jeb answered between bites. "Any man handy with guns, who can sit a horse, can learn with long practice."

"Pete Kitchen is a dead shot," the boy bragged. "He's out hunting Apaches right now. Perhaps another war party. My patrón has killed more Apaches than any man in Pimeria Alta. He was born in Kentucky. Where were you born, señor?"

"In Kentucky."

"I might have known. Have you met my patrón?" the boy asked, eagerness in his question.

"Yes. I have met Pete Kitchen," Jeb said uneasily.

The death chant of the Apaches came up from below the thickening shadows of dusk. The dull thud of a war drum sounded in cadence to the off-key wailing chant, the slow throbbing pulse of a dying Apache, heavy and ominous in the gathering night. From a high pinnacle the tiny blaze of an Apache signal fire showed in the purple twilight. A second fire sprang into being further away, then a third pin-point of light as the fire signal was relayed. The first was blanketed, then the blanket lifted and in a few seconds blanketed again.

"If my patrón was here," Pedrito said, "he could read the smoke signals. I don't like the looks of things."

"The signal fires may be seen by the soldiers," Jeb said, trying to put conviction into the words. "There's soldiers at Camp Lowell. Some will be out on scout detail."

"Pete Kitchen says the soldiers always get there too late," the boy said. "The Apaches always wait till early dawn to attack or when the sun goes down. My patrón will get here before daylight, if he has to ride a relay of horses down and crawl the rest of the way on his belly." There was pride in Pedrito's voice. It was plain the boy's loyalty and love for Pete Kitchen amounted to worship.

Jeb Logan listened while young Pedrito recited the brave and fearless deeds of the Indian fighter. Perhaps

66

the fifteen-year-old boy talked to bolster his own courage during the night's vigil.

An arrow shaft, lighted from barbed black flinthead to feathered tip, raced like a blazing meteor through the black sky and fell downward. It landed on the wide slab, its flinthead buried in the wood, the flaming shaft quivering. The boy smothered the flame with his serape.

When Jeb sighted another tiny flame his rifle cracked. The burning arrow lobbed upward in its shortened flight and fell, striking the ground half way down the slope.

"Pronto," Jeb's voice sounded gritty. "Go below, Pedrito. Bar the doors and fasten the shutters." He hand gripped the boy's shoulder. He pulled one of the Colt guns from its holster and shoved it into the boy's eager hand. "It holds six bullets. Make each one count, boy."

Jeb knew Pedrito wanted to stay up on the roof, but he voiced no complaint as he went down with the gun.

At the foot of the hill the war drum increased its cadence. The death chant became a frenzied, high-pitched scream, as the Apaches worked themselves into the crazed lust to kill. A dozen lighted arrows streaked flame across the sky. All but two fell short. Jeb, using the serape left behind by the boy, slapped the burning arrows out as they struck the planks. The flames from a half dozen arrowshafts along the slope of the hill gave sufficient light to see several Indians crawling towards the house. Jeb fired as rapidly as he could load and jerk the trigger of the rifle, each bullet hitting a human target.

Jeb heard the sound of shots from below and reckoned Pedrito had a long rifle poked through the gun port and was getting in his licks.

Jeb's guns had taken heavy toll. He loaded the rifles and took a long pull at the bottle. He was crouched low, watching as the death chant and the drum beats died out. When the moon pushed up into view, Jeb's teeth bared in a grin. The slope of the hill was bathed in a pale light that revealed the dark blots of dead Apaches. Jeb was seeking that one dead redskin who had almost knifed him, but the maimed body was no longer there. Since his body had been removed under cover of darkness, Jeb figured he must have been some Apache Chief.

Jeb was thinking this Apache Chief must have taken

his money belt from Fay Wayne. It could have been fastened around his middle that was torn away by the horse's hoofs. But to hell with it, Jeb thought, and pulled the corncob stopper from the neck of the mescal bottle and took a drink. He felt the chill of the winter night and wrapped the serape around his shoulders, shrinking into its warmth as he sipped coffee. He had no way of knowing how long the peaceful silence would last. If it held until daylight he was in for a long, tedious wait. Recalling his guerrilla days, he knew this sort of waiting, surrounded by danger, had always been far worse than action, but he'd toughed it out more times than he could remember and under far worse conditions, when he had been empty-gutted, wet and chilled to the bone, exhausted and aching in every muscle; when he would have given all he had to lose for a hot meal and a warm bed and a big drink of rotgut. Hell, he had all the comforts a man needed right now and an itching, healing back to keep him awake.

Jeb conjured up the picture of Mona Durand and the warmth of her red-lipped mouth, the feel of her arms around him. He kept his thoughts on her with an almost frantic concentration, but in spite of it the other girl crept in. Someday, some night, Jeb's hands would tighten around the fat, soft neck of Major Sherwood, and he'd tell the craven son of a bitch why he had to die slowly, so that he could take the cowardly memory of the golden-haired Fay Wayne into hell with him.

Jeb got to his feet, the long rifle cradled in the crook of his arm. He walked around the plank walk-way, trying to shed the black brooding thoughts.

When Pedrito topped the ladder, he looked into the muzzle of Jeb's gun. "Sing out after this, Pedrito," Jeb said gruffly.

"Doña Rosa sent up some hot food," Pedrito said. "She said for me to stay here on guard while you rested. We could hear you walking around."

"I am sorry I kept you awake."

"There is no sleep for any of us with Apaches near," said Pedrito. "And Eduardo is dead," he added, sadness in his voice.

The boy launched into some tale of Pete Kitchen's gun

68

prowess and Jeb listened without interruption to the saga of hero worship.

The rest of the night passed without further attack. At the first sign of daybreak the boy went down to attend to the horses. He was back in a short time, bringing a pot of hot coffee with him.

From somewhere in the distance, where the shadows of night held reluctantly, came the liquid notes of a bugle.

"Too late," the boy said, his words bitter. "Always the soldiers get here too late."

Jeb nodded grimly. It was time for him to move on before the soldiers got here. He had no wish nor intention of being arrested and taken back to Tucson. He finished the coffee.

"Those blue-coated soldiers," he told Pedrito, "have no love for me because I am a Confederate, so I must be moving on. You will convey my gratitude and thanks to Doña Rosa for the food." Jeb started down the ladder.

"If my patrón is with the soldiers, he will take your part," Pedrito said.

"It would only cause trouble, Pedrito."

Jeb saddled quickly. He shook hands with the boy before he mounted.

"Surely you will return, señor?"

"*Quién sabe?* Who knows the answer of tomorrow?" Jeb said, and left it like that as he rode away into the first light of a new day. If Pete Kitchen rode with the soldiers, Jeb had no wish to face him, to accept the man's thanks.

As he rode down the hill, his horse shying away from the dead Apaches lying in their own blood, something on the slope ahead caught his eye. Leaning from his saddle he picked it up and rode with it in his hand. It was his money belt, dirtied and crusted with dried blood. The money pouches were still filled and he knew that money had little value except as a trophy of victory to an Apache. It was the letter that concerned Jeb, his fingers unsteady in eagerness to unlace the string that fastened the flap of the pouch. He was glad it was still there, untouched. The Apache had substituted a buckskin thong for the missing buckle, broken now by the shod hoofs of the horse. Jeb shoved the belt into his saddle pocket and rode on down the hill and along a dim trail. He heard the soldiers as they called back and forth to one another and he thought he heard Pete Kitchen shouting a welcome as he neared his home.

Strange that Jeb Logan was balked by some sort of barrier that stayed his gun hand against the man whom he was almost certain had shot his father in the back. That barricade of safety surrounding Pete Kitchen had built up during the night. Pedrito had offered Jeb something beyond mere friendship. He had taken Jeb into his heart without the shadow of questioning doubt; Doña Rosa had his name in her prayers. A new born baby would carry his name into manhood. When Pete Kitchen returned home, Doña Rosa would laud Jeb Logan as a true saviour, and the boy would weave a brave legend around him.

Kill Pete Kitchen and he'd destroy something. He'd become a black-hearted monster, disguised in the cloak of a true benefactor. They had made it impossible now for Jeb to kill Pete Kitchen.

It had been a strange visitation, that night's stay at El Potrero, Pete Kitchen's ranch, packed with new emotions unknown and foreign to Jeb's nature, gentler things that had no part in the restless call of high adventure. A baby had been born, its first mewling cry a symbol of the beginning of life. A man had reached a generation's span of life and had died there. A woman had suffered the agony of childbirth and had known the joy of looking at her first born and a lasting sorrow had come to her, the woman a link between life and death.

Jeb Logan had withheld the savage Apache attack and had become an irrevocable part of it all, and they had named the baby boy in his honour, attaching his life to theirs.

8

THE WELCOMING warmth of the morning sun was thawing the chill of the long night's vigil from Jeb Logan's aching, cramped muscles. But the man was scarcely aware of its comfort. There was the distant sound of scattered gunfire that seemed to come from every compass point. The gruesome sight of an occasional dead Apache, who had been scalped, sometimes mutilated in white man's retaliation, added nothing to Jeb's peace of mind as he rode away.

Jeb was searching for some hidden place in the canyons and deep *barrancas*, where there was feed and water for his horse; where he could lie down and stretch out and close his eyes that felt strained from the long, dark-shadowed night; some sheltered place where he could rest and sleep.

The Mexican boy had hung a pair of saddle bags, filled with food and grain for his horse, across the saddle horn. He had rolled the serape and tied it behind the saddle when Jeb had pulled the Apache's knife free of the cantle.

Jeb wanted to lie down in a quiet place and try to work out a plan for the days that were to follow. He had come to the end of his reckoning.

Somehow, Jeb had forfeited his right to kill his father's murderer. He had failed to accomplish that which he had set out to do. He had failed to lay claim to his heritage.

Perhaps if his father were alive, he would accuse his son of cowardice, lacking in courage to avenge his death and claim what was rightfully his. It would undoubtedly mean a long, bitter, drawn-out fight in legal courts and would probably end in bloodshed. Perhaps his father would accuse him of lacking the courage to meet the cold-eyed Pete Kitchen face to face with accusation and gun.

Those were the things, Jeb told himself, that needed careful thought and cold calculation, weighing courage against cowardice in the delicate scale of balance set up by his father.

Right now, as he rode weary in the saddle, nerves worn to raw end, Jeb was too mentally exhausted, too confused in his thinking and reasoning, to cope with the ultimate issue. He bore the burden of guilt heavily with each mile his horse travelled. The distant gunfire had died out as he rode into a box canyon where the cured grass touched the stirrups and water seeped from the rimrock above, trickling down into a natural pool in the granite boulders, where the scrub live oaks offered shade. It was like a wishful dream come true.

Jeb swung down and unsaddled and turned his horse loose to roll and water and graze. He carried his gear into the brush and left it. Stripping to the hide, he waded into the cold water that came belly deep. He rubbed down with his flannel shirt and stood naked to let the sun send its warmth into him. He was standing like that when he heard the nicker of a horse. He grabbed up his clothes and belted guns quickly and dove into the brush as his dun horse answered the nicker.

Jeb had on his hat and pants and boots, the gun belt buckled on, a Colt six-shooter in each hand, when horse and rider came into sight.

It was Bob Leatherwood and he was alone, a grin on his face and his eyes squinted into the sun under a hat slanted across his head.

"Lawdy man," he called out. "But you led me a twistin' trail to follow."

Jeb shoved the guns into the holsters as he came through the brush and greeted Bob with a hearty welcome.

"I just came from El Potrero," Bob said. "First time I ever saw Pete Kitchen when he couldn't talk for the lump in his throat." Leatherwood swung down, his right hand extended. "To shake the hand that held the gun that shot the Apache Chief, Carnicero."

"Carnicero!"

"Carnicero, the Butcher, the Mexicans named him. Pete

72

took his ears. There wasn't enough hair on his bullet torn skull to make a scalp. You rid the earth of the bloodiest Apache butcher that ever wore moccasins."

"He's the Apache who killed the girl," Jeb said. "He had her scalp tied to an eagle feather in his hair. He tried to climb behind my saddle and I shot him. My horse kicked his guts out."

Bob handed Jeb a letter and walked away to put a pair of rawhide hobbles on his horse.

The letter from Fay Wayne. Jeb read, "Dear Jeb: By the time you receive this hasty note I am sending in care of your friend, I will be on my way to California. I have your money belt and God willing, I hope to send every dollar back to you someday. Our hours together will remain always in my heart. God bless and protect you always." It was signed Fay.

Jeb stared into space, remembering the girl, knowing that she had been badly frightened, afraid to face whatever the future held. He knew that someday he'd make Major Sherwood pay for the way he had treated her. Jeb shivered in the warm sunlight. Then he touched a match to the letter, letting it burn to white ashes in his hand.

"You took care of her burial, Bob?" Jeb asked quietly.

"Yes, Jeb, I did," Bob answered, then said quickly, "I got bad news for you, Jeb. I was with Major Sherwood and his soldiers when they found those two soldiers you strung up and whipped. The sergeant was alive to tell the tale, but the other soldier was dead."

"They were both alive when I rode away. A man don't die from a quirtin'."

"He was choked to death with a whang leather string, Jeb."

"You think I did it?"

"Hell, no! That buck sergeant did it, but he claims he saw you do it while he lay there playin' possum. You got any eye-witness to prove the two were alive when you left them?" Bob asked.

"There were a few Pimas around, but they stayed behind the brush. I'm positive they saw it all."

"That's something. Maybe Padre Juan can get the truth out of them, but it'll take time. The Major and his foot soldiers turned back from there, taking the sergeant and the dead soldier with them to Camp Lowell. I came on to El Potrero with Pete Kitchen. We ran into Captain Dennis Slattery and a dozen cavalry troopers about daybreak. They'd wiped out what was left of Carnicero's warriors. Every trooper had a fresh scalp tied to his bridle. They're yankee cavalry, but they know how to fight Injuns. Slattery's a West Pointer and a hard ridin', quick shootin' officer who asks no odds and gives no quarter." Bob Leatherwood uncorked the leather-covered flask he always carried, and drank, wiping a hand across his mouth.

"By now, Jeb, Major Sherwood will have filed charges against you. You'll have to lay low, till Padre Juan rounds up those Pimas. Pete Kitchen told me to follow you and bring you back to El Potrero. Lawdy man, you'd be plenty safe there if you stayed a year or till hell froze over."

"From here on, Bob," Jeb Logan said, "I'm travelling alone. They'll have to catch me before they can try me in any kangaroo court. And they'll have to kill me before they catch me." There was a finality to Jeb's voice.

"You stretch out and sleep on it, Jeb, before you come to any decision. I'll stand guard." Bob proffered the flask but Jeb shook his head.

When Jeb crawled in behind the brush and lay down he heard Leatherwood saying, "Pete Kitchen has Tondro's scalping knife. Said to tell you he took it and left you his. He was curious to know how come you were packin' it. When I told him it was the knife Mona Durand used to cut you loose from the whippin' post, he said it tied in with the latest scandal."

"More bad news?" Jeb asked sleepily.

"Pete said he'd heard Matt Durand had hired Tondro to ride the Butterfield Overland Stage, as gun guard, to prevent Apache raids like the one we saw. Tondro, with his rep as a killer, could throw a scare into the Indians and also any road agent gang."

"What's so tough about Tondro?" asked Jeb.

"Tondro's a bushwhacker killer. But crowd him into the open he'll put up a running fight."

"You said once that Pete Kitchen ran him out of the country. Now he's back?" Jeb lay on his belly.

"That's what bothers Pete. He figured Tondro'd never have the guts to come back, but now he has the protection of Durand, which also means Major Sherwood and his soldiers. It don't smell good to a man like Pete Kitchen."

Jeb let the heavy lids come down across his aching eyes. There was no further need to fight off his exhausted need for sleep. The subconscious part of his brain that kept alert filled his fitful slumber with ugly, distorted thoughts, vague disturbing ominous warnings.

The sun had lowered, the shadows of early evening were long, when Jeb finally came awake and sat up with the smell of a mesquite wood fire and the aroma of boiling coffee.

Bob Leatherwood was squatted on his bootheels beside the fire watching the coffee he had brought along in his saddle bags. Jeb washed in the cold water and dried on his shirttail.

"You know any short cuts to Madera Canyon, Bob?" Jeb asked as he sat beside the fire drinking coffee.

"What's waiting in Madera Canyon, Jeb?"

"A grave. It's been waiting there a dozen years."

Leatherwood straightened up with characteristic quick movement, half opening his mouth to voice a question, thought better of it and relaxed again, checking the first word to the other man.

Jeb wasn't quite ready to talk. Those hours of troubled sleep had given him some sort of decision that had not had time to shape itself. He needed advice but he wasn't at all certain what it was he wanted from Bob Leatherwood and Padre Juan at San Xavier del Bac. One thing he was sure of: He was going to get the telescope. His father had given his life for whatever was in the tube and he wanted to study its contents. Perhaps it was a vain sacrifice in the lost cause of the Southern Confederacy. On the other hand, perhaps something could be salvaged in the matter of the Spanish Land Grant. Padre Juan would know the validity of his claim to the vast La Jornada lands. Leathwood was loyal as hell to the defeated cause of the South. A man had to put his trust in somebody.

"It's a grave," Jeb said, measuring each word as he

decided to talk, "of a man named Colonel Wentworth."

Bob Leatherwood's head jerked up, his eyes hard and bright with keen interest and curiosity.

"The tall, lean, one-armed Confederate, who came out of Sonora with a Negro servant and bodyguard?" asked Bob.

"You knew him?"

"Not personally. It was before my time. About '62, when Captain Hunter and his Texan Confederate Cavalry occupied Tucson. I've heard Pete Kitchen mention Colonel Wentworth. Fact is, he said that blue mule at the Mission was a dead ringer for a big blue mule the Colonel's bodyguard rode."

Jeb felt the muscles of his face stiffen and a cold hardness came into his gunmetal eyes. "What else can you tell me about the Colonel?" asked Jeb.

"He disappeared. Vanished overnight. The Negro was seen riding away, pushing the blue mule hard." Leatherwood's eyes looked into Jeb's then he said, "Pete Kitchen might add something to what little I've told you, if you could jar it loose."

"I know he's dead," said Jeb. "I've found his grave in Madera Canyon and I'm going back tonight to dig up something buried there."

"You want me to go along, Jeb?"

"There's a risk involved. Colonel Wentworth was shot in the back, murdered in cold blood for what lies buried in his grave. I wouldn't ask you to share the danger of digging it up. Just tell me how to get to Madera Canyon, and forget it."

"Hell, you'd get lost before you got off to a start. I got an oversized curiosity bump on my boneheaded skull, a Leatherwood trait. I wouldn't be cheated out of this trip if there was a bushwhacker behind every madera tree in the canyon."

"You don't know what the hell you're talking about, Bob," Jeb said gruffly.

"I've got a rough idea, my rebel friend."

"The man's real name was Wentworth Logan. I'm his renegade son. You have a right to know that much before you throw in with me."

76

"It ain't too much of a surprise, Jeb. In fact, I had it half way figured out. So has Pete Kitchen."

"I was afraid of that," Jeb said. "Not afraid. Suspicious. Whatever you want to call the hunch a man has when he's in danger. How come you and Kitchen arrived at the conclusion I was the Colonel's son?"

"Padre Juan buried a Negro and rode a blue mule into San Xavier Mission, about the time a rebel stranger named Jeb Logan rode into Tucson. Pete Kitchen added it up and told me." Leatherwood kicked dirt on the dying coals. "We should take Pete Kitchen along," Bob added.

"Perhaps he'll show up," Jeb said, "when the sign is right."

Something in the tone of Jeb's voice, the bleak look in his eyes, caused the little rebel to eye him narrowly.

"Just what do you mean, Jeb?"

"Let it go as she lays," Jeb said stiffly. He was already regretting what he had told the little man. "I'm travelling alone from here on, Leatherwood. There's nothing to stop you from riding to El Potrero and spilling your guts to Pete Kitchen. I'm headed for Madera Canyon and any man trailing me tonight is asking for trouble." Jeb turned his back and walked over to his horse. He saddled up and rode off without a word or backward glance.

Bob Leatherwood made no gesture, spoke no word to stop him. He stood there, a small man on widespread, saddle-warped legs, his hat pulled low across his eyes, watching Jeb Logan until he was lost to sight in the gathering darkness. Then he moved quickly. He mounted and headed across the broken country for El Potrero Rancho, his face set and a glitter in his eyes that few men had ever seen there. "Damnit. Damnit to hell!" There was a gritty sound to the little rebel's voice that sounded torn from within where conflicting condemnation came to grips with staunch loyalty and hurt friendship, and a sorely wounded pride.

An outspoken man, Bob Leatherwood despised and condemned silent suspicion in other men. That sort of thing hinted of trickery and treachery that was foreign to his nature. Summing it all up as he rode along, Jeb Logan had inferred that Pete Kitchen had killed his father. But Bob Leatherwood knew that while Kitchen had killed and

77

scalped Apaches, and had killed a few Mexicans, he had never killed a white man to his knowledge.

Bob Leatherwood had been in Tucson about a year and during that time he had heard countless tales concerning Pete Kitchen, already an almost legendary figure. You could hear almost anything about such a man if you had an ear for scandal. Coming down to cold facts, it was none of his concern, one way or another, and by the time he had ridden a few miles, he decided to keep his mouth shut and his hand out of it. It had become a firm conviction by the time he reached El Potrero.

Pedrito met him as he reined up and said, "My patrón is not here, señor. He has been gone for perhaps an hour."

"Which trail did he take, Pedrito?"

"*Quién sabe?* Perhaps the sorrow inside the house caused him to ride off." The boy motioned to a cask of mescal. "I am to offer drinks to the mourners when they come. You care to partake of a cup, señor?"

"Another time, Pedrito. Convey my sympathy to them. I have need of haste." Bob Leatherwood rode away, headed for Madera Canyon. It was none of his affair, he kept reminding himself, even as he went into it. It was none of his business if Pete Kitchen and Jeb Logan shot it out. Damnit to hell, and let it alone, Leatherwood. He cursed in a waspish voice, knowing that it did concern him and his code of loyalty to both men.

He pushed his horse to the limit, getting the utmost miles in the shortest possible time, thinking perhaps he could get there in time to prevent a shooting scrape. He knew there was nothing he nor any living man could do if Pete Kitchen bore the guilt of murderer and the son of the dead colonel was in Arizona Territory to avenge the death of his father.

9

Jeb Logan rode along El Camino Real, sometimes called Pete Kitchen's Road to Tucson, Tubac, Tumacacari and Tohell, and before he had travelled a mile on the dust-powdered, rutted road he knew he was being trailed by a man skilled in tracking down Apaches. Whoever it was, he was an old hand at the game. Pete Kitchen was that breed of man.

Jeb used every trick and dodge he had ever learned and when he had wasted too much valuable time trying to catch the man trailing him, he gave it up as a hopeless job and rode on. When he reached the side road he figured led to Madera Canyon he turned off boldly, a gun in his hand.

Hours ago and miles back Jeb had begun to regret his hot-headed, quick-tempered split with Bob Leatherwood. The little rebel had been the only man in Tucson to shove out a hand in welcome. A feeling akin to shame knifed him as he recalled his parting words to his friend.

That was what riding with Quantrill's Guerrillas did to a man. It turned him into an outlaw with a bounty on his hide, trusting no man, not even himself. It made a coyote out of a man who had learned to fight and run and dodge, holing up by day and on the prowl of a night.

As he rode into the wooden canyon, he felt the danger closing in on him like an unseen stealthy thing that made no sound. He spotted the grave by the marked rock slab as he rode in behind a heavy brush thicket and swung down. From his saddle scabbard he took a machete and started digging into the hard-packed ground around the edge of the granite rock slab. He worked with a desperate urgency, figuring it would take a man following him a quarter, perhaps a half hour to slip up within gun range.

In spite of the chill of the winter night sweat beaded his face and he breathed hard and fast through his mouth as he worked against time, watching, listening, nerves taut. He had gouged out a hole, arm deep, when the point of the machete hit metal. Almost flat on his belly now he shoved both arms into the hole, digging his fingers into the moist earth until his hands closed over the round tube, working it free. It was wrapped in a ragged square torn from the Negro's waterproof poncho and the rubberized material had insulated the brass tube against excessive corrosion.

While Jeb was still on his belly, both arms deep in the hole, a shot smashed against his eardrums a split-second after he felt the whining snarl of a bullet that kicked fresh dirt beside him. Jeb jerked up out of the hole, dropping the telescope as he pulled his guns free. A second shot blasted, and somewhere in the brush fifty yards ahead a man let out a harsh scream. The brush thrashed and cracked with frantic movement and a moment later shod hoofs pounded as a rider came at a galloping pace.

Jeb remained flat, the hammers of both his guns thumbed back. He hadn't fired a shot. Someone else had smoked the bushwhacker out and put him to headlong flight.

"Jeb!" The waspish voice of Bob Leatherwood cracked like a whip.

"Here, Bob," Jeb called out. "Lay low. There may be more than one."

"Reckon not." Bob Leatherwood walked across the clearing and squirmed through the brush on the far side where the bushwhacker had been.

Jeb pulled the telescope out and got to his feet, brushing himself off. When Bob came towards him he had a hatband about three inches wide in his hand. It was made of plaited black hair, woven tightly, the ends tied into brushed tufts. Jeb had seen hatbands, quirts, headstalls and bridle reins made of plaited horsehair, dyed brilliant colours to form patterns, but he knew this was human hair and that it must have taken quite a few scalps to make it.

Jeb wanted to ask a question but didn't dare. Perhaps

it showed in his eyes, for Bob Leatherwood said, "The bushwhacker wasn't Pete Kitchen. He don't go in for this sort of thing." He pulled a faded bandana from his hip pocket and wrapped the hatband in it, knotting the four corners together. "You got what you came after, Jeb?" he asked.

"I got it."

"Then let's get the hell gone."

They rode back the way they had come. The telescope lay across Jeb's saddle between his lean belly and the fork.

"Whichaway, Jeb?" Bob asked when they came to El Camino Real.

"I'm headed for San Xavier Mission," Jeb held the telescope up. "I'm taking this to Padre Juan to assay its value."

"I'll go along with you, if you don't mind," Bob said. "When you pulled out I rode to El Potrero, aiming to put a direct question to Pete Kitchen, but he wasn't there. When I picked up the horse tracks following you into Madera Canyon, I thought it was Pete, but when I got a split-second look at the bushwhacker, I knew it wasn't Pete." Bob patted his saddle bag, saying, "For my Confederate money it was Tondro, and I think this hatband will clinch it." Leatherwood scowled into the shadows of night ahead and added, "I'd give something to find out where Pete Kitchen went when he left his ranch."

"That goes double," Jeb said.

"You still figure he had something to do with the murder of your father?"

"I'd give a hell of a lot to be plumb certain he's in the clear, Bob."

"Lawdy man, that was the colonel's killer who shot at you tonight. That puts Pete in the clear."

"Not quite, Bob. Pete Kitchen was in Madera Canyon tonight, but he let his pardner Tondro do the shootin'."

"Lawdy man, don't let you and me go 'round and 'round. Maybe you have more to go on than I have."

"That's right, Bob," Jeb said grimly, his eyes cold. "The Negro saw Pete Kitchen with a *serape* across his shoulder standing with his rifle over my father's body. He was gone before Bugler could get him in his gun sights."

Leatherwood's face had a drawn grey look.

"My father had a forboding of death, Bob. He put it in a letter he gave Bugler to deliver to me." Jeb's hand slapped the brass telescope. "The answer to that pre-meditated cold-blooded murder is inside this tube. That's what I have to go on."

They rode the rest of the way, for the most part, in heavy silence. There was nothing to say when Jeb had finished talking.

A cold white moon rode the sky as the whitewashed adobe walls of the Mission came into view. Late as it was a light showed in the priest's front room window. Jeb dismounted and let Bob take the horses to water and feed.

"*Quién es?* Who is it?" the padre asked.

"The companion of a dead Negro," Jeb replied cautiously.

The door opened just wide enough to show the white-maned padre's weathered face. "Are you alone?" he asked.

"A friend, Bob Leatherwood, accompanies me. He's gone to tend to our horses."

Someone inside the house had snuffed out the light. The room was in darkness when the priest let Jeb in. His caution smelled of danger and Jeb's hand was on his gun butt.

Padre Juan stepped outside and closed the door, leaving Jeb inside in the dark.

The bluish-green flame of a sulphur match was held in a cupped hand over a candle wick. The flame showed Mona Durand standing there, a faint smile on her pale face, her eyes dark-shadowed.

Jeb stared at her as his hand came away from his gun and he slid the door bar in place. Mona was the first to speak. She said, "Major Sherwood and his soldiers are starting out at daybreak to shoot Jeb Logan on sight. There's a hundred dollar reward posted for your capture, dead or alive, for the murder of a soldier." Her voice was a vibrant whisper.

Jeb smiled thinly. "I figured my pelt was worth more. I'm disappointed," he said, contempt in his words.

"This is no time for bravado." Her eyes had angry glints. "I risked a lot to come here to warn you."

"I fully realize that." Jeb's eyes flicked a glance at the engagement ring on her finger.

"I should have stayed home, where I belong." There was a brittle edge to her voice.

"You're right." Jeb eyed the ring contemptuously, then reached out suddenly and took hold of her left hand. "That ring cost the major a lot of money. Down payment on the price he's paying Matt Durand for his daughter." He let go the hand quickly and reached for the door latch. "Go back home. Either marry the man or quit him." He held the door open and let her walk out into the night.

Fighting his anger he heard her ride off at a hard lope for Tucson. He was still white-lipped and shaking inside when Padre Juan and Bob Leatherwood came in a few minutes later.

". . . like a bat outa hell," Leatherwood was saying, "and the devil ten jumps behind. She's a horse woman."

Padre Juan picked up the telescope from the table where Jeb had put it. He examined it closely, giving Jeb a chance to recover his self-composure, before asking about it.

"That telescope," Jeb explained, "has been in the Logan family for generations. My father used it for a map case. I dug it up from under the granite slab that marks his grave in Madera Canyon. Perhaps we can get the big lens unscrewed without causing too much damage."

Padre Juan opened a medicine cabinet and selected a bottle of alcohol. Mixing it with water in a gourd dipper he scoured the telescope with a brush until the brass gleamed. It took a while to get the threads of the brass cap loosened.

The waterproof tube had preserved the parchment land deed and the paper map. Jeb used his six-shooters to hold the map in place while Padre Juan hooked on a pair of steel-rimmed spectacles. His eyes glinted with a strange excitement as he studied the map with the name of the original owner of the vast Le Jornada Land Grant. A man named Esteban de la Guerra.

The deed was in black lettered Spanish script, the capital letters in scarlet. Padre Juan read it aloud:

"From the rising of the sun to the setting thereof, the

leagues travelled on horseback by Lieutenant Estebán de la Guerra, numbering seventy-five miles, measures the square block of land in the unknown wilderness of New Spain and the designated portion known as Pimeria Alta. The grant of land will be known as La Jornada, meaning a day's horseback ride. The ride was made by a gallant Spaniard who, in the end, gave his life. A day's work for a scribe to humbly record a brave Spanish soldier's sacrifice in the name of God and his country. The La Jornada Grant is hereby recorded in the name of Estebán de la Guerra and his true heirs and is to remain in his family as long as there lives a blood ancestor."

There was a gentle smile on the priest's lips and sadness deep in his brown eyes when he said, "In spite of this, the once vast La Jornada Land Grant has slowly disintegrated; perhaps through greed and carelessness. It has been sold and bartered or taken by violence, bit by bit, until little or nothing remains of the original deeded land." He removed the guns and let the old parchment roll back into shape.

"The true deed to La Jornada," Jeb spoke without bitterness or regret, "is therefore worthless."

"As money is counted," Padre Juan held the rolled parchment in his hands, "it has no value."

Jeb took his father's worn-edged, blood-stained letter from the money belt he had laced around his middle under his shirt, and handed it to the priest. "Put this in the telescope along with the rest of my father's heritage. It has the same identical value." He looked at Bob Leatherwood and said, "A man in outlaw boots, Bob," a grin on his mouth, "travels best alone."

Jeb turned and went out. When Bob Leatherwood made a move to follow, the priest motioned him to stay. Holding the telescope to the light, he read aloud the engraved words he had just noticed on the brass.

"Honour above life—Jebediah Logan, Buccaneer."

"This must have belonged to a sea captain named Jebediah Logan, who sailed the Spanish Main under the black flag of piracy," the priest said with interest. Then he put the tube in a desk drawer.

Jeb rode away with a compelling urgency inside him that was akin to panic, as if an unseen danger was at his back, driving him into the night. It was not fear of any living enemy that drove him. It was the two men he had just left, the look in their eyes, the pity and the sympathy along with understanding, the whole of it woven into loyalty and friendship that was his for the taking. Jeb Logan wanted that from no man on earth. He had need of no man's charity.

Something of the same mixed feelings had prompted him to send Mona Durand away with a brutality and cruelty he had forced himself to use against a woman for the first time. Jeb had seen the strange look in her eyes when the priest had closed the door, leaving them alone.

As the candle flame revealed it, naked and unashamed, it was like the fulfillment of a man's hungry dreams through lonely years. She belonged to him. He had only to reach out and she would be his. While he had stayed in the shadow, his back to the door, all the hunger and longing for a good woman's love, all the hurts of boyhood and manhood, the lonesome ache of the years, had come to the surface for the woman to see and heal with her softness and understanding. All the need of man for woman had been in the shadowed grey eyes of Jeb Logan and Mona Durand. But before the candle light had touched Jeb's eyes, betraying all that was inside him, he had shoved it back, knowing that unless he stood straight and clean and proud, free of any taint, he had no right to claim this girl.

Before daybreak he would be on the run, dodging and twisting, looking back across his shoulder like a lobo wolf with the hound pack closing in for the kill. This thing was not for Jeb Logan, nor could it ever be. He had had that one brief glimpse of what the fulfillment of happiness could mean, then he had blinded himself and felt the burning, searing pain that went into his soul and left his eyes glazed.

Jeb did not know that Mona Durand had ridden to Padre Juan's hoping to find Jeb Logan and warn him of danger; to go with him wherever he went, to share his life no matter what the future held. She had told the priest she was mating with a hunted man if he would have her. With the Mexican border a few miles away they'd be safe there, and she had asked Padre Juan to marry them, not giving him a chance to dissuade her as she pleaded their cause.

Until Jeb had lifted her hand, Mona had completely forgotten she still wore the ring of a man she despised and hated with a horrible loathing. She slid the ring from her finger and put it in her pocket as she rode back along El Camino Real to Tucson, her eyes smarting and itching from tears she held back, riding dry-eyed, her head held proudly, carrying a feeling of numbness with her to the house of Matt Durand.

10

JEB LOGAN let the dun horse pick its own trail. Darkness hid the greyish black whiskered mask of his face, the flat metallic look in his eyes as he rode without direction, heedless of any danger that might lie in ambush. His was a black, brooding frame of mind, ugly and isolated, cut off from every vestige of hope and zest for living, as the relentless, lowering ebb of depression crept into his thoughts to destroy whatever wishful hope had been inside him.

He was wholly unaware of the storm building up behind him in the night, the raw wind that pulled a shroud over the stars, to cover up the pale moon and leave a dark pall across mountain and desert and the valley of the Santa Cruz. When he felt the cold wind crawl across the healing welts on his back, he untied the serape and wrapped it around him, flinging one end over his shoulder, Mexican style. When the wind slashed rain at him he hunched his shoulders and lowered his head, pulling his hat down.

He did these things from instinct, hardly realizing the full fury of the storm, only the annoyance of it. When the rain turned into hail that pounded and bruised, the horse under him found what meagre shelter the brush afforded and bushed-up, rump to the storm, while the man sat hunched in the saddle. The hailstorm was of short duration, turning to wet sleet, part rain, part snow, with the night wind behind it.

Jeb almost welcomed the physical discomforts, the shivering chill that relieved his mental agony. For the first time he realized he was hopelessly lost. And now he put all his reliance and faith in the dun horse as he had often done before. Jeb had lost all track of time and

87

distance when he caught sight of a dim yellow blob of light ahead in the drizzle.

He worked the numbed fingers of his hands, slapping them along his chaps to get the circulation started. Since he did not know his whereabouts, the lighted house might hold danger that called for gun play.

The horse took him along a wagon road to a closed pole gate, marked on either side by a pair of whitewashed high adobe pillars. A six-foot wall of adobes and rock extended on either side of the gateway for a dozen or more feet.

Jeb leaned sideways from the saddle to pull the wooden gate pin and when he shoved the gate open a large bell fastened on top of a high arch, commenced a loud clanging. The horse snorted, spooked a little, Jeb sharing its alarm, knowing that the bell had warned of his approach. When he shut the gate the bell stopped ringing.

He had a gun gripped in his hand as he rode towards the house. The light came from a lantern inside an iron grillework fixture at the top of the arched doorway, inside a whitewashed adobe entranceway. There was a huge door of wrought iron, twisted into intricate pattern, fitted with a large Spanish lock, barring the dimly lighted recessed entrance with its worn red Mexican tile floor. Beyond was a massive door with deep carving, in which was set a small barred window about twelve inches square.

Jeb reined up at the long hitchrack about twenty-five feet from the low-roofed, rambling hacienda. The black storm hid horse and rider. Jeb saw the wooden shutters in the peephole of the inside door slowly open, but he couldn't make out the face peering into the storm.

"*Quién es?*" It was a woman's voice that challenged him. "Who is it?" There was fear and alarm in the question.

"I became lost in the storm," Jeb gave reply in the Mexican tongue. "I wish only shelter for myself and my horse. I promise you have nothing to fear." Jeb put conviction into the words.

"Ask the *yanqui* his name, *nieta*." This time it was a man's voice, an old voice, harsh with suspicion.

"Your name, señor?" the granddaughter questioned.

"Jeb Logan. I am a stranger here."

"*Madre de Dios!*" the girl's voice shrilled. "Señor Jeb

Logan. The name of the man I described, Don Joaquín!"

"Perhaps it is a gringo lie," spoke the grandfather.

"It is easily proved, Don Joaquín," the girl said softly. Then in a louder tone she called to Jeb. "Ride into the light, señor, to prove your identity."

"To be shot from the saddle," Jeb said derisively. "What hombre is in the house to make identification. What enemy, perhaps?" His voice held grim mockery.

"It is I who will identify you, señor," the girl explained excitedly. "If you are Jeb Logan you will remember, perhaps, the girl who opened the door for you at Pete Kitchen's."

Jeb Logan was chilled to the marrow of his bones. If this was a trick to kill him, a man dies only once. He rode into the yellow blob of the lantern, a gun in his hand. At sight of horse and rider the girl let out a small cry, with a sob caught in it.

"It is truly Jeb Logan! *Madre de Dios!* It is the one!"

"You are alone, señor?" questioned the grandfather, suspicion gone from his voice.

"I am alone."

"You will find hay and grain in the stable. When you have cared for your horse, my house is yours, Señor Jeb Logan."

"I will go with him," the girl said. "I will take the lantern."

A moment later the girl, with a serape over her head, led the way. She had the barn door open by the time Jeb swung from the saddle. She hung the lantern on a rawhide rope that swung from the ridge-log, and while he unsaddled, she brought grain and spilled it into the wooden box fastened to the manger, then forked in hay. Save for a small roan Spanish mule the ten-stall barn was empty.

Taking off the serape the girl stood before Jeb in a gay-coloured fiesta dress. Jeb watched her as he kicked off his chaps. She was small, with large dark brown eyes, lips parted to show white teeth, and very young.

"That is a beautiful dress on a beautiful señorita," Jeb complimented her.

"It is New Year's Eve, nearing the midnight hour," she said shyly. "I must not leave Don Joaquín alone. He is blind. He is dying inside the Hacienda del Jornada. I am afraid." She pulled the serape around her.

"Hacienda del Jornada!" Jeb said with astonishment. "What is your grandfather's name?" he asked.

"Joaquín de la Guerra," she replied. "A proud name from Spain."

Semidarkness hid the bewildered, uncertain grin that stiffened Jeb Logan's cold muscles along his stubbled face, as he followed the girl to the house, entering by way of the kitchen.

The warm, sweet odour of the kitchen reminded him that he had not eaten for a long time. The red coals from an open oven shed a red glow and Jeb moved towards its warmth. Somewhere a clock chimed, deep-toned, striking the hour of eleven.

"Make haste, Consuela!" Don Joaquín called from another room. "Show Señor Jeb Logan to his room. Its last occupant was a Colonel Wentworth. You have perhaps heard the name, señor." There was a strange excitement in the quivering voice.

"Colonel Wentworth was my father, Don Joaquín," Jeb answered.

"He spoke of his son, Jeb Logan. Make haste to join me. I have much to tell you concerning La Jornada."

Consuela took Jeb's hand, leading him along a candlelit hallway. She opened the door and crossed the room to light a candle and touch the flame to the fire laid in the fireplace in a far corner.

She had a quick, lithe way of moving, as a dancer moves lightly, sure-footed. She opened the doors of a tall wardrobe, where half a dozen suits hung. Charro jackets and pants tailored from soft glove leather; large sombreros and low-crowned Spanish hats with stiff brims and a half dozen pairs of boots.

"These clothes belonged to my father, Esteban de la Guerra." Consuela's smile was gone now. "He was called Steve at Tucson and Tubac. He was gay and gallant and brave, a true *caballero*. He was killed when I was but a child but I remember him well."

Consuela crossed the room to where Jeb was standing. She reached up and kissed him quickly, saying, "The Señor Dios has sent you here, even as he sent you to

El Potrero." She was gone before Jeb regained his composure.

Jeb stripped to his wet skin and rubbed the rough bath towel over his cold body till the chill was gone. He put on the charro suit Consuela had laid out on the bed, boots and dry socks, underwear, a shirt of heavy white silk, a crimson tie that matched the red silk sash. It was like dressing for a masquerade ball, Jeb thought. Steve de la Guerra must have been his size. Even the boots fit.

Jeb shaved with the dead man's razor and admired his reflection in the long mirror with a twisted smile, wondering how many times Steve had stood before this mirror, with the same smile, the same look in his eyes.

He heard the girl open the door behind him and saw her image reflected in the mirror. Consuela held a lighted candle in a tall, silver holder. He could see the soft smile at the corners of her mouth, the shadowed look in her large brown eyes that turned them into soft black, deep pools. Somewhere he remembered an old half-forgotten superstition that told of romance in this scene. He felt the quick pulse of blood in his veins as he tried to recall the words that went into the picture that would pledge them in some superstitious vow of love.

Even as the girl's lips moved, the big clock bonged the half hour, its mellow echo sounding through the silence. The candle light guttered, flamed once, then went out as if blown by a breath beyond the dark hallway. The blood drained from Consuela's flushed face, leaving it pale with a nameless fear darkening her eyes.

Jeb turned quickly and crossed the room, grabbing the candlestick as it slid from her hands. She was trembling as if stricken by a sudden chill. He held her for a long moment.

> "Wish on the candle flame
> And you shall see
> Mirrored there, the man
> Whose bride you shall be."

Jeb heard the whispered words he had tried to recall. "The breath of death," Consuela said against his shoulder, "blew out the candle."

91

"It was a draft from the hall, child," Jeb told her, leading her down the hall.

The living-room of the old rambling house, with its three-foot adobe walls, was approximately fifty feet square. Enormous, handadzed beams of Mexican mahogany supported the ceiling. A series of old Spanish tapestries in rich dark reds, greens, ochres and oranges, depicting the saga of Don Quixote and Sancho Panza, in life size replica, hung from ceiling to tiled floor to cover the aged and yellowed whitewashed walls. No trace of rug or carpet covered the worn red, dull polished tile floor. Every piece of furniture was massive, heavily carved and waxed, hand rubbed to velvet smoothness. Large high-backed arm chairs were embossed with leather, studded with brass nails. There was a long refectory table with matching chairs and a massive sideboard piled with beautifully etched and polished silverware.

A fireplace burning four-foot cordwood logs, supported on massive andirons, was the only light in the large room.

Above the fireplace was the life-sized oil portrait of a handsomely arrogant Spanish soldier mounted on a coal black horse of Arab strain. It was the work of a true artist who, with bold heavy strokes, had captured something in the soldier and horse, portraying it on the canvas. Time had darkened and mellowed the painting, shadowing it with the years.

In the dull red glow from the yule log suffusing the room, the painting came to life with subtle, invisible movement. There was a contemptuous set to the thin-lipped, cruel mouth. The face itself revealed nothing, neither fear nor reckless courage, betraying no trace of emotion. It was a mask put on the face of a young soldier going into battle; a young soldier dedicated to war from birth with a military training to discard fear and face danger without flinching. It was there in the arrogant tilt of the head as he sat the restive eager black horse with the sleek tensed muscles and flared nostrils that had caught the smell of danger.

Deeply etched into the silver plate at the bottom of the black oak frame was the young soldier's name, Estebán de la Guerra.

Jeb Logan, standing in the doorway, reluctantly turned his attention from the portrait and as he looked into the eyes of the living man, Joaquín de la Guerra, the painting of his famed ancestor was quickly forgotten.

Jeb, sucking in a quick breath, froze in his tracks. In that moment he understood the fear inside Consuela de la Guerra, the granddaughter of this man who stood like some apparition of death itself. Joaquín de la Guerra was a fleshless skeleton, dressed in a charro jacket and pants made of soft black glove leather, the heavily embossed silver-threaded decorations dulled and tarnished. The crimson tie had the appearance of a wide ribbon of blood down the front of the white shirt, and the wide crimson sash around his thin waist gave him a garish, macabre look. A rusty, black serape with ragged fringe lay over his shoulders and arms.

There was no sign of flesh under the yellow, dry parchment skin stretched taut across the high-bridged, aquiline nose and high cheek bones. There was no hair on his bald yellow skull, and the shaggy snow-white eyebrows looked like tufts of goat hair glued to the parchment skin above the hollow black sockets of a pair of sightless eyes.

Once Jeb looked into those eyes he couldn't take his gaze away. The lids had long since shrivelled and withered into the skull, and the eyes appeared like flat, oblong discs.

Jeb felt the presence of the girl in the shadowed hallway. She was standing so close he could feel her quick breath on the back of his neck.

"Señor Logan is standing in the hall doorway, Don Joaquín," Consuela told her grandfather. "He is unarmed."

"I am aware of the señor's presence." The voice had the brittle sound of dry leaves crushed in a man's fist. For the first time, Jeb was aware of the cloying odour of death that permeated the room, seeping into corners and dusty crevices.

The serape slid down, hanging limply from the old man's hunched shoulders. He held a pistol in his two skeleton hands. The gun was held on the level of the crimson sash, the long barrel pointed steadily at Jeb Logan's belly.

Jeb felt the clammy sweat beading his forehead as he watched the metallic sheen of the blind eyes.

"If you are truly the son of the one-armed Colonel Wentworth Logan," Don Joaquín's voice deepened with some stifled inner emotion, "you have nothing to fear under my roof, señor. But what proof do you have?" he asked.

Jeb felt the hot flush of annoyance. The angry frustration was betrayed in his voice when he spoke. "I left what identification I had with Padre Juan at San Xavier del Bac, if you will take the word of a priest."

"What was the nature of your identification, señor?"

"The original deed to the La Jornada Land Grant, written in Spanish script, naming Esteban de la Guerra as the original owner. It has been buried for a dozen years in the grave of my father in Madera Canyon." Jeb recounted the full story to the old man.

"There is no need for further proof," Don Joaquín said, placing the gun on the mantel over the fireplace. "Forgive my lack of hospitality and this armed display of suspicion, señor."

"It is understandable, Don Joaquín."

"I am handicapped by the infirmity of old age and blindness. An old Pima called Coyote tends to my needs and guards the gate, but I sent him to enjoy the holiday fiestas with his relatives. El Coyote should have returned today. Perhaps the storm has delayed him." The worn teeth bared as he clapped his fleshless hands together with a bony sound.

"Consuela," he called, "fetch the brandy from the large barrel in the wine cellar." The skeleton hands made a gesture. "Be seated in a chair near the fire, señor."

Jeb's boot heels clicked as he crossed the room and sat down opposite the living skeleton, who had seated himself in a big arm chair facing the warmth of the fire.

The clock ticked loudly as Don Joaquín spoke in a rasping, conspiratorial whisper. "Each swing of the pendulum, señor, brings me nearer to death that comes to all men. Youth squanders time with a prodigal hand. Old age hoards each second with rudeness." He cocked his head sideways, listening to make sure the girl had not returned.

"Would you consider taking my granddaughter in marriage, señor?" he asked bluntly.

The question caught Jeb off balance. "Consuela is but a child, Don Joaquín," he said, "while I am a grown man of thirty-two." Jeb felt the heat in his face and squirmed under the blind scrutiny.

"Your father and I discussed it when he purchased the La Jornada from me," Don Joaquín said, a certain finality in his words. "A dowry of twenty-five thousand in gold, the purchase price of La Jornada, is included."

Jeb, feeling trapped, wiped the sweat off with a white linen handkerchief. Turning his head, he saw the girl standing motionless in the doorway, a bottle of brandy in her hand. She had taken off her high-heeled slippers and stood in bare feet. The blood had drained from her face and a stricken look was in her eyes.

"I will abide by the wishes of my dead father, señor." Jeb faced the old Spaniard, each tick of the clock hammering at his eardrums.

Don Joaquín leaned a little forward, thrusting his head on scrawny neck into the hot glow of the fire. He spoke from there. "Then it is agreed," he said tonelessly.

Jeb heard the girl suck breath into her parted lips.

"Nieta," the aged man spoke without moving, "fill the silver goblets with brandy. To pledge the agreement."

Jeb watched Consuela slide her feet into the slippers and walk woodenly across the tiled floor, her lithe young grace now gone. Filling the massive goblets on the sideboard, she put one in her grandfather's outstretched claw. The other she gave to Jeb as his hand closed over hers. He smiled into her pale face and leaning over, he kissed her lips that felt cold and lifeless.

Consuela slid her hand free and turned away quickly, leaving the room as if in full flight from terror.

Jeb, the goblet filled to the brim in his hand, felt pity saturated heavily in his heart, while he fought back anger for the old Spaniard's ruthlessness.

Don Joaquín had risen from the chair and stood facing the fire, his sightless eyes fastened on the portrait, his mouth a cruel line.

"The last of the de la Guerra women," the words came through his tight lipless mouth, "pledged to Señor Jeb

Logan." As he lifted the goblet, Jeb stood up and they drank with the pledge.

Jeb felt the smooth warmth of the very old brandy as it went down his throat and into his empty belly, absorbing the chill that was there. Then he put the goblet on the arm of his chair and crossed the room in long, swift strides. He almost ran down the dark hallway to the closed door of Consuela's room.

Without the formality of knocking, he opened the bedroom door. Consuela was kneeling on a stool of worn padded leather in front of a recessed niche in the thick adobe wall. A votive candle burned at the foot of a small wooden statue of the Blessed Virgin in a blue robe.

"Your grandfather," Jeb told the girl, lifting her to her feet, "acted according to his code. He wished only for the security of the grandchild he is leaving behind."

The girl was rigid in Jeb's arms, when she said, "That painting of Estebán de la Guerra and his La Jornada land have taken the place of God in this house. There was no thought of happiness for me."

"You are a beautiful girl, Consuela. Any man would be proud to claim you in marriage and make you happy," Jeb tried to choose the right words.

"That makes no difference to Don Joaquín. He pledged you to a lie that binds you to eternity. I would rather die than be a part of that horrible bargain."

"Would it be that bad, Consuela?" He forced a grin, holding her when she fought to free herself. "Let Don Joaquín die believing the pledge is binding. After he's gone and buried, it will be time enough to decide."

Jeb held her face in his hands until the strange look was gone from her dark eyes, his grin forcing a pitiful smile to her lips. Then he kissed her gently and the warmth of her mouth returned the kiss.

His arm around her slim waist, he led her back to the big room. Don Joaquín stood with his back to the fire, the old serape draped about his shoulders, as Jeb had first seen him, the red glow across the blind eyes. The skeleton arms made a gesture. "Hola!" he said. "The final minute of the old year is at hand! Fill the goblets, Nieta."

The two men, one in the prime of life, the other aged, dying, held the silver cups. Don Joaquín again faced the portrait of the Conquistador, the goblet lifted. As the two men drank, the deep-toned bong of the clock struck the hour of midnight and echoed like the tolling of a funeral bell in the silent house.

11

THE LAST echo of the passing of the dead year was gone. Don Joaquín held the emptied goblet in his hands as he stood motionless, parchment-dried face lifted, blind eyes fixed on the painting of Don Estebán and the horse he had ridden to mark the boundaries of La Jornada. Tears welled from neglected, shrivelled tear ducts, quickly blotted as they coursed unchecked on dry skin.

When the old Spaniard resumed his seat in the high-backed arm chair, Consuela took the goblet from him and moved away, motioning Jeb to be seated on the other side of the fireplace.

"The name de la Guerra," Don Joaquín spoke, "means war. The men of de la Guerra blood were all soldiers, who fought for glory and in the end died bravely. The spoils of war rightfully belong to the soldier, but there was none to be had in the barren wasteland of mountains and waterless desert.

"The fabled Seven Cities of Cibola, supposedly rich in solid gold and silver, were a myth. The futile expedition of conquistadores led by Captain Francisco Vasquez de Coronado, proved the worthless value of the land. The seven mythical cities proved to be Indian pueblos on high, barren mesas."

Don Joaquín went on to tell Jeb Logan the same story Padre Juan had recounted about Coronado's young Lieutenant Estebán de la Guerra volunteering to carry the message of his defeat to the City of Mexico; about the land he was given, marked by a pile of rocks at the end of his first day's journey; how he had died at the hands of hostile Indians; about the cross Coronado had made out of his broken sword and stuck in the rock pile when he had found the lieutenant days later. He told how the Hacienda del Jornada was built later around the rock monument.

The old Spaniard rose slowly, his hand reaching to the mantel for the broken sword that was on the shelf. Holding the cross in his skeleton hands, he said, "It is my wish that it be placed in my coffin." He laid it gently back on the mantel and resumed his chair, continuing his story.

"The ancestors of Don Estebán, being soldiers, sold their allotted lands within the boundaries of La Jornada for a few pesos to the agrarians who came with Padre Kino. Land was of no value to a soldier fighting the wars of Mexico.

"As the oldest member of the de la Guerra family left alive, I rightfully claimed this original hacienda. I lived here with the last of my five sons, the one I named Estebán, after the conquistador. When his wife died, Consuela was left in my care. Estebán drank heavily and gambled in Tucson and Tubac and without my knowledge he used the Hacienda del Jornada as collateral for the notes he signed. When a gringo named Matt Durand demanded payment, my son killed himself.

"Colonel Wentworth Logan came shortly afterwards, paying me twenty-five thousand in gold for this hacienda, and I gave him the original Spanish Grant as a receipt, signing my rights of ownership over to him with the understanding that I occupy La Jornada as long as I lived. After I died it was to belong to your father and his heir.

"Your father said his life was in great danger and that Pete Kitchen was to guide him and the Negro servant over a safe trail into Sonora. When I left I buried the gold under the old brandy barrel in the wine cellar. It was not yet daybreak and as I entered the kitchen door I was struck down from behind by a man who had come in the back way.

"When I came awake he was standing over me. A large man whose breath stank of whisky. He demanded the gold Colonel Wentworth had paid me. I told him there was no gold; that the Hacienda del Jornada belonged to me and to no other man; that my son had no right to gamble it away."

Don Joaquín passed a skeleton hand across his eyes

99

and continued talking. "The big man was drunk and abusive. He went outside and brought in a broken branch of a cholla cactus in his gloved hands. He stood over me and made his final demand and when I spat my refusal in his face, he stabbed the cactus into my eyes. He left me unconscious with the spines sticking from the blinded eyes.

"It was Pete Kitchen who found me and sent to Tucson for a doctor and to the Mission for Padre Juan." Don Joaquín stopped talking.

"Who was the man, Don Joaquín?" Jeb asked.

"A scalp hunter named Tondro, in the employ of Matt Durand."

Jeb filled the two goblets and handed one to the old man who had risen from his chair, to stand erect, his sightless eyes on the portrait. He lifted the goblet like a silver chalice.

"Jornada de la Muerte," he whispered. "The Journey of Death."

Jeb lifted his drink in tribute to the man in the painting and in salutation to the man taking that last journey.

The emptied goblet slid from the skeleton hands and Jeb caught the old Spaniard before he fell. Lowering him into the high-backed chair, he knew that Don Joaquín was dead.

Jeb pulled the old serape over the dead face with a strange feeling of unreality, as if living in a dream, the red glow of the fire furnishing artistic lighting effects.

Consuela placed a lighted candle on either side of the black shrouded man sitting in the chair. "I feel no grief, no sorrow," she said. "A disrespectful thing."

"You have lived with this too long," Jeb said kindly. "The black dress you changed into is sufficient respect."

"A custom." Her eyes looked at him. "You are absolved from any pledge, Jeb Logan."

Jeb put his hands on her shoulders and looking into her eyes he said. "This has always been your home, Consuela. It will remain your home. One day you will fall in love with a young man of suitable age."

"There will be no one but Pedrito, whom I have always known."

"Pedrito!" Jeb said. "You mean Pedrito who calls Pete

Kitchen his patrón?" he asked, counting the years until the boy would grow into manhood.

"In three years," Consuela said, as if reading his thoughts, "Pedrito will be eighteen." Colour suffused the girl's pale cheeks. "We have discussed our marriage."

"A splendid thing. I share your happiness."

The distant clamour of the gate bell came through the storm. Consuela made a small, frightened cry as she pressed close to Jeb. "It is not the old Pima called Coyote. He unties the rope before opening the gate. Who then? There is danger."

Jeb left her and went down the hallway, returning with his cartridge belt and guns. "Whatever happens," he warned her, "stay hidden in the house. I'll welcome our visitor." There was a grim promise in the words as Jeb buckled on his cartridge belt.

Jeb cautiously pulled the shutters of the small opening in the front door. The lantern light inside the iron grille fixture sought to penetrate the storm-filled black maw of the night. Jeb welcomed the blast of wind-driven rain in his face to clear his brain. He slid the long barrel of one of his guns between the open iron work for an un-hampered shot.

When he saw the blurred shape of horse and rider move at the end of the lantern light, he thumbed back the gun hammer and waited. He voiced no challenge, checking it to the visitor.

"Consuela!" The black wind whipped the words. "Don Joaquín! It is Pedrito!"

"Ride into the light."

"Who speaks?" Alarm and suspicion was in the question.

"Jeb Logan. If you are Pedrito, we are not strangers."

An inarticulate cry came out of the storm as the rider spurred his horse into the light. Jeb saw the pinched cold face of the Mexican boy and called Consuela to come unlock the door.

While Consuela took Pedrito into the house, Jeb swung onto the boy's horse and rode to the barn. He fooled around after he had cared for the animal, wanting time to think things out, to see where he stood. He was glad to be out of the old house with its traditions, its death

101

and sorrow. Small wonder the young girl was filled with dread, living with it and a part of it. A hell of a depressing thing that stifled laughter. There was something depraved about it; the dying subsisting off the living, repaying it only after death with a bride's dowry, passing on the guardianship to a stranger. And yet that insidious thing had its justification in the sightless eyes of old Don Joaquín.

Who, after all, was Jeb Logan to pass judgment? What the hell had he done? He'd gotten here in time to watch the old Spaniard die, to put in his claim for the girl and La Jornada. Marry the girl and get the price paid back for the land grant: A young, beautiful bride and twenty-five thousand dollars.

That could have been how the blind, dying old Spaniard had sized up the situation. Take a good look at yourself, Logan, before you pass judgment on the dead. Better put Jeb Logan into the foreground where he belongs, dressed just as he is in a dead man's clothes, his belly and gut full of a dead man's grub, his brain a little drunk and twisted by too much of a dead man's brandy. Step into that picture, Jeb Logan, then back away and let's have your honest, unbiased opinion, taken as a whole. Masterpiece or damned fake. Let's have it, Logan, now you're playing God Almighty. Get it out of your system before you leave the sanctuary of the barn and go back to that house where you received true hospitality; where a dying man played host and you acted out the courtesy that becomes a guest.

Either that, or saddle up, Logan, and get the hell gone and don't set foot again on the La Jornada. *Vamos, gringo!*

Jeb had been standing in the stall alongside his dun horse, fighting his bitter, almost maudlin, wordless soliloquy, his eyes fastened on the partly open door. It was pitch dark inside and Jeb had not seen anyone slip in but somehow he became aware of the presence of another person here in the darkness. He froze in his tracks and slid his gun free.

"Señor," a whispered voice called. "Señor Jeb." It was Pedrito.

"*Qué pasa?* What is wrong, Pedrito?" Jeb asked, wondering why the half-frozen youngster had forsaken the warmth of the fire to come here. He stepped out of the stall. "*Qué hay,* boy?"

"Consuela sent me to warn you of danger, señor. It was there beneath the arched gate that I collided with the *espíritu* of Don Joaquín, señor. No more than naked flesh in flight, wet from the rain, with cold death in the skin, suspended in the air as it brushed my face in flight. My horse snorted and as I lifted my hand, it touched the espíritu.

"It was only when I found out that Don Joaquín was dead that the strange encounter had an explanation. I thought it was only his espíritu, but when I told Consuela about it, she hastened me to tell you."

"Go back to the house, pronto," Jeb told Pedrito, knowing the inbred superstition of the Mexicans. "See that all the doors and windows are locked and the shutters fastened. There is grave danger here, but it is alive. It's no ghostly apparition lurking in the night as you think, boy." Jeb shoved Pedrito through the barn door with a slap of comradeship and said, "Go now, and I will investigate the gate."

Jeb remained standing in the barn door until Pedrito was inside the house. The fury of the storm had spent itself. The wind was tearing the black clouds to shreds. Patches of stars showed and a cold white moon pushed a lopsided prow through the black clouds like a battered boat in high breakers.

Jeb closed the barn door and sloshed his way through mud and slush. A flat grin pulled his mouth into a grim line, his slivered eyes were murderous, knowing it was no ghost in mid-air flight that the boy had collided with.

Jeb could make out the ghoulish thing hanging from the arch of the gate as the wind buffeted and twisted it, swaying the weight at the end of a rawhide rope. A wholly naked dark-skinned dead Indian, with a shock of sodden black hair in ropelike strands covering the face. The tongue had been yanked out by the roots and now hung by a buckskin string tied around the neck to make a gruesome necklace.

Jeb prowled the underbrush cutting for sign, but the storm had covered all traces of the killers. The Indian had not been scalped. He had been stabbed in the back

103

and chest and stomach, like slits in wet brown leather.

Jeb went back to the house, leaving the dead Indian hanging there.

"It was an Indian, stabbed many times," he told Pedrito. "His tongue was cut out and hung by a string around his neck. Perhaps for a reason I do not understand."

"It is because the tongue talked, señor," Pedrito explained. "The Apaches have ways of punishing their own kind. It is one less Apache on earth, señor. I go to look at the hanged one. It does not upset me to see a dead Apache."

Jeb stripped and rubbed down and put on his own dried-out clothes. He pulled on his damp boots before they dried and hardened. He was drinking hot black coffee when Pedrito came back.

"It is no Apache, Señor Jeb. It is the old Pima called Coyote. He was among the Pimas who watched you quirt the two soldiers. He told Pete Kitchen about it."

"That was the reason for ripping out the tongue," Jeb said, tasting the bitterness inside his mouth. "I am the cause of Coyote's murder." Jeb put on his hat and hitched up his gun belt. He was going to cut the Indian down and take him to his jacal behind the barn.

It seemed to Jeb that death tracked his every step; that the omen of bad luck clung to his back with sharp claws.

News had a way of travelling rapidly in Indian country. Sunrise found a dozen Pimas, relatives and friends of the murdered Coyote, gathered around the humble jacal. Pedrito, who had a knowledge of the language, talked to them as they dug a grave and prepared Coyote for burial.

"The murderer of old Coyote," Pedrito told Jeb, "was the soldier you tied to the tree and quirted. The killing took place at a Pima hogan where Coyote and his companions were drinking pulque. The body was brought here and hung to the gate as a warning to other Pimas who might talk too much."

"Tell them," Jeb said grimly, "that the murderer will be punished."

"I have already told them that my patrón and you will attend to it. Those Pimas who were with Coyote and witnessed your quirting of the soldiers have already departed for the Mission to tell Padre Juan."

"They possess courage, Pedrito."

"Pimas are peaceful. But men nevertheless. The murder has aroused their anger. I told them to tell Padre Juan about the death of Don Joaquín and I sent one to El Potrero to take the sad news to my patrón. Doña Rosa will be here before noon to assist Consuela."

"You have a level head for such matters, boy."

"I have had to attend to such things before, señor."

"Will Pete Kitchen accompany Doña Rosa?" Jeb asked.

"No. The Señor Doctor will not permit it."

"Doctor! Has Pete Kitchen been wounded?"

"He was taken ill without warning. He tied himself in the saddle and his mule brought him home. He was wet with cold sweat and in great pain when I put him to bed. The Señor Doctor says it is an organ in the body called the gall bladder. He is taking pills but whisky is forbidden. A hardship for my patrón."

"Where did this sudden illness take place?"

"In Madera Canyon where he followed the scalper Tondro. It was like a knife, my patrón said. The pain so intense he fell from the saddle and at daybreak he crawled back on his mule and the animal brought him home. The patrón wishes his illness to be kept a secret."

"I will not mention it to anyone, Pedrito," Jeb assured him.

"You will be Don Jeb of La Jornada, señor," Pedrito said proudly. "I would like to be your vaquero, perhaps your majordomo when I am old enough." There was sincerity in the boy's eyes and the quiet tone of his voice.

"I am glad you think I would fit in here, Pedrito. When you have finished school and you and Consuela are married, this will be your home, and someday, you will be Don Pedro of La Jornada."

"Gracias, señor," Pedrito said happily.

Jeb saddled his dun horse, telling Pedrito he would be away on business for a day or two. He was halfway to the gate when a troop of cavalry rode through. The half dozen horses and soldiers were mud-plastered. Jeb's teeth bared in a flat grimace as he dropped the bridle reins across the saddle horn, both hands resting on the pair of guns. If this was Major Sherwood, he hoped Sergeant Burch was among the lot.

But the officer in charge, unlike Sherwood, sat his horse as if he belonged in the saddle. His men were seasoned troopers, hard-bitten, their unshaven faces lean and weathered. The tails of their horses were plaited in heavy braids and tied up to keep them out of the mud. They wore their hats with the jack-deuce slant of a cavalry man and while their blue uniforms were soiled, the guns and heavy cavalry sabers were spotlessly clean in saddle scabbards.

Jeb recognized the Irish Captain, Dennis Slattery, as he rode in the lead, a few days growth of sandy red whiskers bristling along his jaw. His gloved hand was raised in a careless salute and his squinted eyes flicked a look at Jeb's guns.

Ignoring the threat of Jeb's hands resting carelessly on the gun butts, Slattery reined up. Eyeing Jeb he said, "We bivouacked a few miles from here last night, sir, with a jug of Pete Kitchen's whiskey and a quarter of his beef, to celebrate the New Year. We've been on the prowl for Apaches. We cut sign of moccasin tracks that led here."

"Pima tracks." Jeb made a quick decision. "I'm Jeb Logan," he said, watching the other man's eyes.

"I'm Captain Dennis Slattery," came the quick reply.

"Let's lay 'er on the line, Captain. Major Sherwood posted a bulletin at Camp Lowell, offering a reward for the capture of Jeb Logan."

"I neither read, nor am I governed by the bulletins of Major Sherwood. My outfit is no longer quartered at the camp. Two of my troopers are following with pack mules and with the owner's permission, we'd like to pitch camp here for a few days."

"The owner, Don Joaquín de la Guerra, died early this morning," Jeb said, his hands no longer on the gun butts. "He was an old man. His granddaughter is alone in the house."

"In that case we will move on." Captain Slattery would have reined around to leave but for Jeb's gesture.

"You and your men are welcome to what La Jornada has to offer," he told Slattery. "There's stall room in the barn for your horses, hay and grain."

"That's damn hospitable, but. . . ."

"A rebel named Jeb Logan has inherited this Hacienda

del Jornada." Jeb's hard-lipped mouth twisted in a sardonic grin. "Rebel Don Jeb welcomes you as my first guests. A squad of damn yankee cavalry. That's one for the book, eh Captain?"

Captain Slattery grinned, twisting his head to tell his sergeant about the dead owner and that they would camp here.

"There's a dead Pima named Coyote who lived here and took care of Don Joaquín," Jeb said as they rode towards the barn. "He was hung to the arched gateway by some white men." Jeb went on to tell about the stabbing and hanging, and why it had taken place and how it involved him, in regard to the dead soldier, Smithson.

"I will be glad to talk to the Pimas who are here and do all I can to clear you of the murder charge, Logan," Captain Slattery said after he had listened to the story.

"Pedrito!" Jeb called to the boy who was inside the barn.

"Qué hay?" The Mexican boy's voice was shrill with suspicion. "You are a prisoner of the Yanqui soldiers, no?"

"No," Jeb spoke quickly as he caught a brief glimpse of Pedrito in an empty manger, hidden all but the top of his head. He had seen the gun he held steady on the side of the manger, one eye squinted shut, the other lining the sights, the barrel pointed at Slattery's belly. "Put the gun away, Compadre. Captain Slattery and his soldiers are guests. They will camp here for a few days."

Pedrito shoved the gun into its holster and climbed out of the manger. He eyed the soldiers as he went past. Jeb had told him to go to the house and tell Consuela there was no cause for alarm.

"Whew!" Slattery let out a gusty sigh of relief. "The lad meant business. Does he live here?"

"No. Pedrito lives at El Potrero Rancho. His father and mother were killed by Apaches. Pete Kitchen gives the boy a home."

"It is brutality such as this that makes a man hold with General Crook's belief that the only good Apache is a dead one," Captain Slattery said grimly.

"I was on my way to El Potrero," Jeb told Slattery, "when you arrived. Unless you need me here, I'll ride along."

"There is nothing to hold you here," Captain Slattery said. "I shall talk to the Pimas and try to get the true facts of the soldier's killing and why old Coyote was murdered."

Jeb shook hands with the Captain and rode to the house. He said goodbye to Consuela and gave Pedrito instructions to take care of Captain Slattery's needs.

12

WHEN JEB sighted the mule-drawn spring wagon with Doña Rosa and a half dozen black shawled women on their way to La Jornada, he reined his horse off the rutted El Camino Real and into the brush, riding wide around them. He had no desire to meet the wife of Pete Kitchen right now.

It was perhaps an hour later that Jeb let the dun horse climb the hill to Pete Kitchen's house. There was nobody around. The ranch was deserted and he had come up within easy gun range when he heard Kitchen's voice hailing him from an open window. The long barrel of a rifle shoved across the window sill glinted in the morning sunlight.

"Put up your horse, Logan. I'm laid up with rocks in my gizzard."

Jeb unsaddled and put his horse in a stall in the barn, filling the grain box with cracked corn and barley. He unbuckled his spurs and kicked off his chaps, leaving them on his saddle. Pete Kitchen's horse was the only other one in the barn.

Jeb hitched up his gun belt as he stood there trying to figure out what he would say, then decided he'd check the bet to Pete Kitchen; let him open the jackpot. This was the big showdown with the man who had killed his father.

He closed the barn door and sloshed through the mud to the house. Remembering the scrubbed floor, he scraped his boots on the iron scraper outside the kitchen door, finishing the job with an old broom. He lifted the latch and went in.

"You're shore as hell house-broke," he heard Pete Kitchen's chuckle. "There's a jug on the kitchen shelf. Fetch it along. Doc Hand's put me on the Injun list. No booze or I'll swell up like a poisoned dog. Hell, a man's as good as dead when he can't hold likker."

Jeb carried the jug to the bedroom. There was the smell of medicine saturating the room. Pete Kitchen was propped up by pillows on the bed that had been pushed near the window. The rifle lay on the wide adobe window ledge. A sawed-off shotgun leaned against the wall, and a cartridge belt and holstered gun hung from the bedstead. On a table within his reach was an Indian basket filled with rifle cartridges and shotgun shells loaded with buckshot, along with a bottle of medicine and a pill box.

Pete wore a white nightshirt. His face, with a week's stubble of whiskers, had a yellow-jaundiced look. The man had lost a lot of weight. Suffering lined the yellowed face.

The forced grin of welcome slacked as Jeb ignored the hand Pete held out.

"What's on your mind, Logan?" Kitchen asked, his eyes narrowed.

"I came to Arizona Territory to kill the man who murdered my father," Jeb said. "A one-armed Colonel Wentworth of the Confederate Army, whose full name was Wentworth Logan. He was murdered about twelve years ago and the description of the killer fits Pete Kitchen."

"You don't strike me as a man who would wait for a feller to be laid up flat on his back, to go gunnin' for him." A sardonic grin worked a crooked line along the Indian fighter's bloodless lips.

"I didn't come here to kill you. I came to find out the reason why you killed my father."

"Then you aimed to go away, leavin' the job undone?" The thin smile twisted upward at one corner.

"Damned if I know," said Jeb.

"How come you changed your mind, Logan?"

"A woman called Doña Rosa, and a kid named Pedrito. They changed my mind," Jeb said flatly.

"That sounds odd," Pete smiled, "comin' from a Quantrill Guerrilla."

Jeb felt uncomfortable under the scrutiny of the sick man's eyes.

"By Almighty God," Pete Kitchen shook his head with

110

its sweat-dank mat of hair. "I never killed your father. I wouldn't lie about a thing like that. You got my word for it, my hand on it." The arm in the white sleeve came up from under the blanket.

This time Jeb crossed the room to grip it. It was like some hard twisted knot inside him had broken loose without warning, spilling out a hot flow into his cold belly and guts, more potent than any liquor ever stilled. The blood pounded into his throat, pulsing there. It was a while before he trusted his voice.

"By God, Pete Kitchen!" It was all he could manage to say.

"That goes double, Jeb Logan." Pete lay back against the pillows, sweat beading every pore, his lips pulled back, his eyes squinted with pain and nausea, as the sick man fought back the black waves of dizziness.

Jeb saw the shaggy head lop sideways, the taut muscles relax as the man went limp. Jeb slid the pillows out and lowered the head to a natural position. He dippered cool water from a red clay olla into a tin basin, found a sponge and wet the yellow face and sweat-matted hair. He held the dipper to the open lips, letting the water trickle slowly into the mouth. After a while the man swallowed and opened his eyes, looking at Jeb with a glazed stare, devoid of recognition. Jeb read the labels on the medicine and managed to give the sick man his hourly dosage.

Jeb pulled a chair alongside the bed and watched the jaundiced face, his hand on the limp wrist, feeling the feeble pulse beat. It looked as if Kitchen was dying under Jeb's helpless eyes, and he wanted this man, above all men, to live. He cursed inwardly at his impotent inability to lend some of his own vitality and strength to the sick man who so badly needed it. Doña Rosa's absence annoyed him. Her place was home tending to her sick husband. Jeb transferred his abortive anger to the doctor who had left Pete Kitchen to die with only a bottle of foul smelling medicine and a box of pain killer pills.

Jeb looked at the sick man and his one-man arsenal. A hell of a way for an Apache fighter, the notorious Pete Kitchen, to die, sick, and at the mercy of his enemies.

The thick-walled adobe house sat on top of a hill.

111

Jeb looked out the window to the slope where he had stood off Carnicero and his war party. He examined the rifle and shotgun, putting each gun back in its place. There was nothing he could do for the sick man until it was time to give him another dose of medicine, so he tiptoed out of the room to the kitchen.

A large coffee pot and a couple of big iron dutch-oven kettles sat on the back of the stove. The coffee was strong and hot and when he lifted the lids of the pots he found them filled with meat and beans, swimming in thick red chili sauce. A pan of sourdough biscuits was in the warming oven. Jeb filled a plate with food and carried it and a cup of coffee back to the sick room.

Pete Kitchen had propped himself on one elbow and was reaching for the holstered gun with a groping hand. Sweat glistened his skin and his eyes were without focus as he muttered incoherent sounds from behind clenched teeth.

Jeb crossed the room with quick strides. He put the plate and cup down on the window ledge and gripped Pete's arm that reached for the gun. "Lay back, Pete," Jeb said quietly, "take it easy."

"Who the hell are you, hombre?" Pete's eyes tried to focus.

"Jeb Logan. I came to ride herd on you. Remember?" Jeb eased him back on the pillows. He sponged the sweaty face and head and when Pete lay quiet Jeb ate the food and carried the empty plate and cup to the kitchen, returning to the sick room to resume his vigil.

Pete Kitchen had said he had not killed Jeb's father and Jeb was more than satisfied to take the man's word, content in the truth of the statement without outside proof, in spite of the fact that the Negro had given Jeb a complete description of Pete Kitchen as he saw him standing over the one-armed colonel's body, a smoking rifle in his hand, a serape across his shoulder. Jeb knew from his personal knowledge of the man that Kitchen was not a bushwhacker murderer. It showed in every trait of his character.

Watching the sick man now, Jeb, who had been wary of close friendships, wanted him for a friend. Jeb had always known that a man with a price on his head could not afford the friendship of any man. One careless word and that comradeship would be betrayed. He had lived a dozen years by the outlaw code that decrees "trust no man but yourself and watch yourself as you'd keep an eye on an enemy, lest you betray yourself through some weakness like booze or the love of a woman or a misplaced friendship in a man". Those things tended to soften a man till his tongue unlocked the secret hiding place where he kept his thoughts. Those were the red flags of danger that were never lowered. An outlaw's very existence depended on his constant wariness and awareness.

Jeb stared out the window without vision, his eyes turned inward on brooding, bitter thoughts that went back along the trail of years, to turn up the stumbling stones along the way where the regrets had been buried; torturing himself with the mistakes of his life; stifling all self-pity; trying to evaluate it in cold retrospect; salvaging anything worth keeping; discarding the rest as worthless. This was the end of the trail. La Jornada. The end of the journey. The fulfillment of a man's destiny.

At first the incoherent mutterings of the sick, delirious, perhaps dying man were disconnected words without meaning. Jeb spooned medicine down the man's throat on the prescribed hour and fed him the small white pill when he writhed in pain, and sponged his face. Jeb was too consumed with his own confused thinking to pay attention to the muttered words, until gradually they seemed to take on meaning, and Jeb became aware that Pete Kitchen was making a fight for his life. A hell of a fight against big odds.

Pushing his own thoughts aside, Jeb fought along with him. "I'm here, Pete. It's Jeb Logan, Pete. I'm here beside you, Pete." Jeb kept talking to reassure the sick man.

After a long while Pete's jaundiced eyes opened and he said, "I know you've been here quite a spell, ridin' close herd . . . Doc gimme one chance in a hundred when he left. I bet him a Philadelphia hat I'd make a live of it. I'm cuttin' the odds down. . . ."

"You sure as hell are, Pete." Jeb answered the question in the sick man's eyes, hoping they wouldn't detect the grave doubt. "Your colour's better. I'm no doctor but

I'm givin' you an even chance for your taw." Jeb tried to assure him.

"All a man needs is a fightin' chance. I'm tough as a boot." He lay back, closing his eyes.

Sometimes Pete would lie motionless, his eyes squinted shut, summoning his strength. Then his eyes would open and he would talk for a little while, but always he was aware of the sound of Jeb's voice as he talked to help him make the fight to live.

Jeb told him about the Negro dying from an Apache arrow in the back; about the brass telescope he'd dug from his father's grave and what it contained; about the death of old Don Joaquín; about Consuela and Pedrito; about the murder of old Coyote, and the reason why.

Jeb was sure the sick man was listening, that what he was telling him was helping him as much as the medicine, and he watched the face for any change of expression, until finally the colourless lips spread in a grin.

"Ain't you left something out, Jeb?" he asked. "I mean Mona Durand."

Jeb felt the red flush that came into his face, the muscles along his jaw tighten. He said, "I left her out on purpose, Pete."

"She'd make you a good wife, Jeb," Pete said. "Girls like Mona don't run in bunches."

"Like as not I'll shoot Matt Durand down where I find him," Jeb said. "I know now it was his hired killer, Tondro, who murdered my father. I don't need to explain further why I can't marry his daughter, even if she'd have me."

"Reckon not, Jeb. But it's a damned shame it can't be different."

Jeb filled the spoon with the medicine and Pete made a wry face as he swallowed it, saying it tasted like dead skunk. He lay back on the pillow. After a while he said, "The La Jornada land was split into seven chunks. Your father bought six of them, one at a time, with Confederate money, allowing the owners to stay on the land until he was ready to take possession. The seventh piece of land belonged to Don Joaquín de la Guerra and it was rumoured that your father visited the old Spaniard and left a bag of gold with him but nobody knew for sure.

114

When the war was over the Confederate money was worthless so the six men still claimed ownership. Then when Matt Durand showed up and wanted the La Jornada, he hired Tondro to murder the six owners after making them sign over the lands to him.

"But it would seem to me that your father had a prior claim to the six pieces of land he paid for in gold and obtained titles to. He gave up his life for this and it's up to his son to play his hand out."

"That's what my father had in mind," said Jeb. "That's why I came to Arizona Territory; to claim the heritage he left me, and to kill whoever murdered him."

"That's goin' to be a tough job," said Pete Kitchen. "And the odds stacked against Jeb Logan."

"Don Joaquín sold my father the Hacienda del Jornada but kept it a secret. He was to remain on the place as long as he lived, according to the agreement. The old Spaniard told me all about it before he died. I am now the rightful owner of the Hacienda del Jornada and the other six pieces of land that make up the original grant. That's worth fightin' for, Pete."

"Your father would want you to fight for it, Jeb," Pete said, then added, "I'd come up out of Sonora to meet him and the Negro in Madera Canyon at midnight. I was delayed dodgin' Apaches, and when I got there your father was dead. I took a snapshot at the killer as he rode off but missed. The man was Tondro. I took in after him but lost the trail. When I got back the Negro had buried your father and pulled out."

"The Negro saw your smoking rifle," Jeb said. "He thought you'd done the killing."

"I found out later that the Colonel's real name was Wentworth Logan," Pete went on to explain. "And that he had a son Jeb who was a Captain in Quantrill's Guerrillas. So I held back and waited till you showed up. It took a long time but you've finally come." Pete lay back, exhausted, a faint grin on his tight lips. "I'd seen the Negro on the big blue mule and when I saw the mule at the Mission, I knew it was the same mule the Negro had ridden away . . . a long time ago."

Jeb stood by the window. The lowering sun sent dark shadows into the barrancas and canyons of distant mountain ranges and broken foothills. A wind-swept cloud like a long gossamer scarf trailed in the wake of the golden colour of the sun above the dark purple mountains that cut a saw-toothed pattern against the sky. The slanting rays found a thick growth of manzanita, polishing the rain washed red bark of the branches and the thick green leaves. Its last rays touched the peaks in a parting salute as the day ended in a golden blaze of glory. The hush of the twilight had fallen as if the unseen hand of God had blessed the day.

It was the brief pause when time stood motionless, the Angelus hour when men on earth thanked God; when the song birds gave voice; when the timid whitetailed deer came to water; when riders dismounted, unsaddled, and turned their horses loose. A peaceful hour on earth with the lull of silence in it.

Jeb was aware of it all, the breathtaking cathedral beauty, the restful hush in the afterglow of sunset, as he stood staring into the far distance, his eyes darkened with memories of almost forgotten yesterdays.

Jeb closed the heavy shutters and turned to look down at Pete Kitchen with concerned eyes, fearful of the death that lurked in the shadowed corners of the room. He had watched too many men die.

"You're tough as a boot, Pete," Jeb spoke harshly, annoyed with death and its ethereal black shroud. "You're too tough to die in a peaceful bed, Pete." He bent over in the dim light for some sign of a grin on the sick man's taut lips, a flicker of an eyelid, but the sallow, greyish-yellow mask was devoid of expression.

"You picked a hell of a time to kick the bucket," Jeb said with annoyance. "Leaving a man in a tight." An unreasoning anger swelled inside Jeb as he swore meaningless words until he got it all out of his system. "And to hell with it," he finished and turned away.

He found Pete's jug and gulped down the corn liquor. He hung a faded old serape over the window and lit the lamp, turning it on low wick. There was about three inches of medicine left and he fed it to the sick man with a trickle of water for a chaser. "Swallow, damnit, before you choke," he growled, watching the adam's apple in the corded throat move.

Jeb picked up the rifle and shoved a handful of cartridges into his pocket and picked up Pete's watch from the table. He pulled his hat down on his head as he went out, saying, "And see to it you don't die off till I get back." Jeb thought he could detect the twitch of a grin on the tight-pulled lips.

He watered and fed the two horses, then went up on the roof with a pair of field glasses he'd found on the ktichen shelf. The moon had come up and Jeb scanned the country below with the glasses, watching for sign of movement in the brush. He watched some cattle for a while, knowing that even gentle cattle, used to men on horseback, will quit grazing to watch a rider with bovine curiosity, and that a man on foot will spook range cattle accustomed to horsebackers. But there was no sign of anyone afoot or on horseback.

Jeb lowered the glasses, pulling the chilly, clean air into his lungs. He hoped Pete Kitchen had heard his cursing, a language he could understand and relish, taking strength from the profanity.

Pete had told the doctor from Tucson to get the hell back to town, because his just being here couldn't help a man who was kicking the bucket. He'd make a live of it or die, one. Rocks in his damn gizzard. A hell of a note. Gall bladder out of kilter and the bile sliming his belly, coming up his gullet and into his mouth like he'd been on a long drunk.

Pete had gotten rid of Doña Rosa and the womenfolk with their everlasting prayers and tears and sympathy. If his number was up, he wanted to be left alone to play his string out. But Jeb knew that Pete Kitchen was glad he had come, a man who'd take a pull at the jug and talk his language.

Jeb and Pete savvied the same things that couldn't be put into words. It formed a bond and tie that strengthened itself of its own accord. Jeb had felt it there when he first met Pete Kitchen in the barber shop, when he had it made to kill a man of his description with ice in his eyes. He'd had a hard time keeping the hate for Kitchen in his heart, for every time he turned around, every man he'd met, put in a good word for the Apache fighter.

Jeb looked at the watch. It was time he got down

below to see how the sick man was making out. He focused the glasses for a final look before he climbed down the ladder. This time he sighted the cattle that had quit grazing and were moving away from the brush along the bank of the creek close to where the wagon trail crossed. He held the glasses focused until he saw a movement in the brush. With his left hand he laid the rifle barrel along the wooden barricade that was almost breast high, and pointed the gun without aiming at a patch of brush the lenses were bringing close. A black shadow moved out on a narrow strip of sand along the edge of the water and the black blot took shape in the form of a man. Jeb thumbed back the hammer on the rifle and the roar was cannon loud in the silence of the night and the man's scream could be heard as he dived headlong into the brush.

Jeb had not mean to fire at that moment, but the rifle had a hair-trigger and the touch of his finger had fired the gun. "Damn the luck!" Jeb gritted and dropped the rifle and field glasses. A Colt gun in each hand, he raked the brush below with .44 slugs.

He put the guns down and again focused the field glasses. He picked up a man on horseback, beyond gun range, before he rode out of sight. A tall man in the saddle on a dark coloured horse. Then he picked up another rider who sat his saddle like a sack of bran, the man at whom Jeb had taken the unwanted rifle shot. Jeb was willing to bet the man was the heavy set, paunchy soldier, Sergeant Burch, and that the man beyond gun range was Tondro.

Gritting profanity, Jeb ejected the empty shells from each six-shooter and shoved fresh cartridges into the empty chambers. He eased himself down the ladder, taking the glasses and rifle with him.

When he came back into the sick room, Pete Kitchen was sitting up in bed, the shotgun across his lap. There was a wild look in his eyes.

"The battle's over," Jeb told him. "The damn war lost. Why the hell didn't you tell a man you'd filed a damn hair-trigger on the rifle?"

"What the hell kinds guns you used to?" Pete asked.

"There's times when that hair-trigger can mean the difference between life and death. Who got killed?"

"Nobody."

"A hell of a lot of wasted bullets, by the sound of the shooting. Scared the pee-waddin' outa me." Pete Kitchen leaned the shotgun against the wall. "Turn up the lamp, Jeb. I passed a handful of gizzard gravel. Gawdamighty, it hurt! I coulda chawed a railroad spike in half. Doc told me if I passed that load of gravel my gizzard would quit givin' me hell. Anything left in the jug, Jeb? A man givin' birth to a damn rock pile needs a drink." His whiskered yellow face was slimed with cold sweat from the ordeal, his hands trembling.

Jeb grinned wryly as he sponged the sweat from the sick man's face. Pete no longer felt the pain that had for long days and nights been a constant drag. There was only a weakness and aftermath of nausea, and the exhaustion.

Pete's arm made a gesture. "Drag out the chamber pot from under the bed, Jeb. I want to count them rocks. The way I felt there must be a hatful. Doc said to keep a tally."

Pete counted six of the little stones, disappointed in their size. His ice steel-grey eyes were clearing as he stabbed a stubby forefinger at Jeb, saying, "I'll be in shape to fork a horse by tomorrow. We'll be Johnny-on-the-spot at Hacienda del Jornada when big Matt Durand and his gunslinger, Tondro, show up to take possession of the whole land grant."

"You're in no shape to set a saddle, Pete."

"Then hook a team of mules to the buckboard and I'll travel in style along the highway to Tucson, Tubac and Tohell." He managed to put a swagger into it.

"That pot-bellied Matt Durand has been holdin' back waitin' for old Don Joaquín to die. He aims to get hold of that old adobe casa. All you got to do, Jeb, is to marry Mona Durand to get the La Jornada Grant. It'd save lawsuits and bullets."

"I'll take the bullets and the lawsuits, Pete, in the order named."

"That's complimentary as hell to the lady."

"Simmer down, Pete, before you commence passing

119

more gravel." Jeb fed him another pill. "Maybe I'll give you a slug of whisky when you wake up. I'll prowl around for a while and you'd better get some sleep."

Jeb picked up the field glasses and turned the lamp on low wick as he went out to resume his lonely night watch. The winter chill of the night kept him awake as he walked around the plank walkway on the roof. It was a safe bet that Burch and Tondro wouldn't return, but a man had to make certain. He came down every hour to check, but Pete was sound asleep each time, breathing normally, the unhealthy tinge fading from his skin.

He kindled a fire in the kitchen stove and heated the coffee and food. He watered and fed the horses before daybreak when he wolfed a hearty breakfast.

He was on watch on the roof at dawn when he picked up a lone rider with the glasses. It was the Mexican boy, Pedrito.

Jeb met him at the barn.

"Doña Rosa is concerned about my patrón," Pedrito said. "I'm to return with a report of his health as soon as possible."

"The patrón is better," Jeb told the boy. "He no longer suffers pain and is asleep now from exhaustion."

"Padre Juan and Señor Leatherwood are at the hacienda. Señor Leatherwood and Captain Slattery would like you to return as quickly as possible, Señor Jeb." Pedrito told him.

"As soon as Pete Kitchen is awake, we will pull out for La Jornada," Jeb said. "Better go to the house and get some breakfast, but don't wake the patrón, Pedrito."

13

THE MOTHER Superior and two Sisters from St. Joseph's Academy for Young Females at Tucson accompanied Padre Juan to Hacienda del Jornada. Padre Juan rode the blue mule and the Mother Superior drove the spring wagon. Slapping the lines across the rumps of the gentle team of fat horses, she exchanged gentle banter with a dry wit that matched the priest's rare humour.

The nuns were now inside the house with Consuela and Doña Rosa and the black shawled Mexican women, displaying their grief according to the custom.

The paid mourners, a half dozen men who chanted the hymns, were outside, fortified with food and mescal.

Twenty or more Pima Indians kept to themselves as they squatted around the little adobe jacal where the body of Coyote lay in a pine board box. They sat in watchful, patient silence, their opaque black eyes revealing nothing.

Captain Slattery and his handful of troopers had been fed and rested, their gear and uniforms cleaned of the muck.

Bob Leatherwood and Captain Slattery rode together around the place as they watched to see who came through the arched gateway. "That gate," Bob Leatherwood said testily, "has been closed to visitors for a dozen years. Now that Don Joaquín is dead, it's wide open."

"Who's idea was it?" asked Slattery.

"The dead man's," Leatherwood spoke caustically. "It's the Mexican custom to parade grief like the . . ."

"Like the shanty Irish," finished Dennis Slattery.

"Like the Irish," Leatherwood laughed. "Everyone coming to this Mexican wake will console with hushed words the row of weeping women, then will pass into the next room to view the corpse. It was the request of the old

Spaniard, a blinded, bitter man, with an ingrown hatred for mankind, that the long-closed door be opened to his enemies and false friends."

"I don't get it," the Captain shook his head.

"Then you haven't viewed the corpse." Bob Leatherwood, standing in the warm sun, shivered a little.

"You make it sound a gruesome kind of ordeal," Slattery said uncertainly. "I'll forgo the formality. What's the joker, Bob?"

"I never had the doubtful honour of meeting Don Joaquín when alive, but I got a look at him in his coffin. A skeleton with a death's head. His eyes looked into mine. Lawdy man, I liked to jumped through my hide when I looked into those lidless eyes that shine like tarnished metal discs." Leatherwood unscrewed the metal cap to his leather flask and said, "I wish Jeb Logan would get here. Wonder what in hell's keepin' him?"

Captain Slattery pulled a pair of army field glasses from a leather case on his McClennan saddle and focused them along El Camino Real, where almost a mile distant half a dozen rigs of all descriptions had come into view.

"One of the rigs," Slattery said, "is the mule-drawn army ambulance Major Sherwood uses for his private conveyance. He's got a squad of his infantrymen mounted for armed escort. The curtains are strapped down. No telling who rides inside." He handed the glasses to Leatherwood.

"Time to act military, Cap. Line up your troopers on each side of the gateway, sabers lifted in salute as Major Sherwood drives through."

Slattery made a vulgar sound with his sun cracked lips.

"That's Solomon Warner's surrey behind the ambulance," Leatherwood said. "Time was when Don Joaquín and Warner were cronies, according to Padre Juan." Leatherwood let out a grunt. "Lawdy man," he said, "that's rebel Bill Ouray and some of his vigilantes ridin' outpost. What in the name of hell is keepin' that damn Logan!" He swung the glasses to the south where Pete Kitchen's road Tohell came up from Sonora. He choked off the start of a rebel yell. "That's Jeb a-comin' at a high lope, with Pete Kitchen in a rig, pourin' the whip to his span of

122

mules, and Pedrito hangin' onto the seat by the skin of his teeth, both arms full of guns. Lawdy man, Old Man River's beginnin' to rise. If it overflows the bank at La Jornada, God help the women and kids." He shoved the glasses into Slattery's gloved hands.

Unscrewing the metal stopper on the flask, he eyed Captain Slattery and asked crisply. "If it comes to a showdown, Irish, just where do you stand?"

"In the broad middle, rebel," Slattery said grimly. "I could be court martialled and drummed out of the army for the thoughts inside my skull. I have a couple of dirty white chips in this game and the joker up my sleeve."

"You mean this Sergeant Burch deal, Captain?"

"That too. But the joker's the card that will have Major Sherwood sweating blood when the army red tape is cut and tied in a hangman's knot around his fat, red neck." Slattery took the proffered flask and drank.

Jeb Logan rode through the arched gateway just ahead of Kitchen's buckboard that made the turn on two wheels. There was a grin on Pete's face that showed a row of teeth under the drooping moustache. His black and white serape hung across one shoulder and his hat was pulled slanted across his ice coloured eyes. Pedrito held two rifles in his arms. The sawed-off shotgun was in a scabbard alongside the seat. As the rig came through Pete raised the buggy whip in a mocking salute to Solomon Warner, whose matched team was travelling at a sedate pace.

"An apparition," Solomon Warner told his wife on the seat beside him. "Dr. Hand said the man was dying. Pete Kitchen would get drunk at his own funeral."

"Pete is good to his family," Solomon's wife reproved him gently. "No happier wife exists than Doña Rosa. Pete Kitchen is a good man for all his drinking, Solomon."

"Aye. A good man, Pete Kitchen," Solomon agreed. "I will let you out at the door where Padre Juan stands."

"Go lightly, Solomon," his wife smiled, "when Pete offers you his jug at the stable. Who is the handsome rider on the dun horse?" she asked.

"Jeb Logan. The man Major Sherwood horsewhipped. Your woman's curiosity satisfied?" He pulled up in front of the hacienda, cramping the wheel to leave the step free.

Jeb Logan rose alongside the buckboard as Pete Kitchen pulled his mule team to a walk. Pete took the rifles from the boy's arms and told Pedrito to take care of the team. He laid the guns on the seat and got out of the rig.

Jeb, eyeing the ambulance that had halted in front of the house, watched Major Sherwood step down in a formal dress uniform. He sucked in his breath when Mona Durand, ignoring the major's proffered hand, stepped down and walked into the house. She was dressed in a tailored suit of dark grey, a matching grey mantilla over her head.

Jeb caught sight of a man in civilian clothes inside the ambulance as Sherwood got back in, telling the driver to head for the army tents where Captain Slattery had made camp beyond the corrals.

One of Sherwood's mounted infantrymen rode over to where Slattery and Leatherwood sat their horses near the gate.

"Major Sherwood," the soldier said, saluting Slattery, "commands the immediate arrest of the Quantrill outlaw, Jeb Logan, charged with the murder of Private Smithson."

"Tell Major Sherwood that Captain Slattery will report to him personally regarding the matter of Jeb Logan's arrest," the Captain said, and added, "Now get the hell out of my sight."

"Here goes, Leatherwood," Captain Slattery grinned when the soldier rode away. "I'll keep you posted from time to time."

"The luck of the Irish go with you, Captain."

"I can use it, Bob." Slattery's eyes were cold as he rode towards the army camp.

Little Bob Leatherwood rode over to where Jeb Logan and Pete Kitchen were standing in the doorway of the stable. His squinted eyes held a bright, hard spark as he looked down from his saddle at the two men. Jeb grinned up at the little rebel, braced for some caustic remark.

Instead, Leatherwood swung to the ground, unscrewed the top of the flask and handed it to Jeb. "Drink up, Don Jeb of La Jornada!"

Jeb lifted the flask. "Salud!" he said.

They watched the top buggy approach. Dr. Hand pulled

up, a puzzled half-smile, half-scowl on his face as he looked at Pete Kitchen. Pete shoved a hand under his serape and brought out a cardboard pill box, rattling it. "Here's your damned *piedras negras*, Doc. You said to bring them to you. You owe me the best damned Philadelphia hat in Warner's store."

Dr. Hand waited until Solomon Warner drove up in his surrey. "Order a dozen hats for Pete Kitchen, Solomon," he told the store-keeper. "I got a new cure for gallstones. Pete was dying when he ran me off with a shotgun, but I see my medicine cured him." Then turning to Pete Kitchen who was uncorking his whisky jug he said, "I told you to quit that rotgut, Pete."

"Hell, likker never killed a man if he uses good judgment," argued Pete.

"A quart a day isn't good judgment. Don't crowd your luck, Pete."

"Likker up, gents," Pete said ignoring Dr. Hand's warning. "By hell, we'll need fortifyin' when we pass Don Joaquín's coffin. I hope Matt Durand shows up. I'll be right on his tail to see that he takes a long, long look into that old Spaniard's eyes."

"Matt Durand," said Dr. Hand, "left on the stage for California yesterday morning at daybreak, before the news of Don Joaquín's death reached Tucson. He's bringing back Senator Sherwood of California for the wedding of his son to Mona. Here's to the gizzard gravel, Pete," Doc said and took a long pull at the passing jug.

"You feel like losin' another bet, Doc," asked Pete Kitchen, "that that weddin' won't come off?"

"You'll win that bet, Pete," Solomon Warner cut in, taking the jug Dr. Hand shoved at him. He took a quick look over his shoulder at the house before he tilted the jug expertly across his forearm and elbow and took three hasty gulps.

Pete Kitchen jerked a blunt thumb in Jeb Logan's direction and lowering his voice, he said, "Jeb Logan and the granddaughter, Consuela, were with old Don Joaquín when he died. Jeb is the owner of the whole damned La Jornada land grant, in spite of hell, high water and Matt Durand, by God!"

Pete's voice carried to where Jeb, Bob Leatherwood

and Bill Ouray were. Jeb had met and liked Bill Ouray on sight.

"When Pete's voice lowers to what he calls a whisper," Ouray was saying, "they can hear him in Tucson. They'll think it's a voice from the grave. Doc Hand had him dead and every saloon in Tucson held a wake for him. Heaven help Pete when he shows up alive." Bill Ouray took the flask from Leatherwood's hand. "We'll back your claim to La Jornada, Jeb Logan," he said, then drank.

"Lawdy man, look yonder!" Leatherwood pointed towards the gate. The funeral of Don Joaquín was attracting a motley gathering from all walks of life; surreys drawn by matched teams; big cumbersome wooden-wheeled carretas filled with Mexicans; vaqueros on horseback; peons walking barefooted in the drying mud. The men watched the odd procession for a while.

Pete Kitchen joined Leatherwood and Ouray and Jeb. His blunt thumb gouged the small of Jeb's back. He motioned towards the cavalry camp.

The fly of the larger tent was open. Captain Slattery's back was to them as he stood facing Major Sherwood, who was seated on a folding canvas camp stool, at a small table in front of him. The tall, lean man in a business suit stood behind the Major, while the Major's orderly stood to one side, a sheaf of papers in his hand.

Sherwood's face was livid, the pale eyes venomous as he glared at Captain Slattery. "Your refusal to obey orders," he said, his voice out of control, "comes under the head of insolence and insubordination, Slattery!"

"Captain Slattery, sir," the West Point cavalry officer corrected Sherwood.

"That's beside the point." Sherwood banged a heavy fist on the table, scattering a pile of official looking papers. "I repeat the order. Place Jeb Logan under arrest. Fetch the prisoner here." His voice had risen testily.

"I refuse to be a party to petty, vindictive quarrelling," said Captain Slattery. "The framed-up charge of murder against Jeb Logan has been proven false by eyewitnesses, who saw Sergeant Burch murder Private Smithson, after Jeb had left the scene. You have read my report."

"The testimony of a pack of drunken, lousy Pimas. You'd have me put the statements of the gut-eating Indians

126

above the sworn testimony of a white man, a soldier wearing the same uniform you wear! And you a West Point officer! What the hell sort of discipline do they teach at the Military Academy?"

"The manners and conduct, sir, of an officer and a gentleman," Captain Slattery answered, standing stiffly at attention, his spurred boot heels clicking as he saluted in the exact quick precision of the figure four. He held it, waiting for the courtesy of the Major's return salute. When it didn't come, Slattery made an about face and strode, stiff backed, out of the tent.

Slattery's weather-cracked lips were pulled into a bloodless line. Controlled rage had drained the colour from his sunburnt face when he came up to Jeb Logan. Cold anger showed in his eyes when he spoke. "Major Sherwood," he said, his voice brittle, "seems set in his determination to take you back to Camp Lowell under arrest."

"We overheard the conversation."

"Major Sherwood's lawyer read me a legal document that gives Matt Durand title to the entire La Jornada land grant. When the funeral is over, Sherwood will inform everyone here to vacate the premises. He and his new bride are to live here."

"Bride!" Bob Leatherwood said in a low-toned, deflated voice. "Since when . . . ?"

"Major Sherwood was married to Mona Durand in a pre-dawn ceremony, a short hour before her father left for California." Captain Slattery informed them, then reached for the flask in Leatherwood's limp hand. He rinsed the brandy in his mouth before he spat it out. With a wry grin he swallowed the next drink and handed the flask back.

"Leatherwood," Pete Kitchen spoke up, "you and Bill Ouray stay here with Jeb Logan." He gripped Slattery's arm. "Come along with me, Captain," he said grim_y.

Jeb Logan stood there between the two men. The news of Mona's marriage had left its impact.

Halfway to the tent, Pete Kitchen spoke. "I'm acting for Jeb Logan, Cap. You willing to second Major Sherwood when I put it up to him to fight the duel?" he asked.

"It will be a doubtful honour, Pete. But a hell of a pleasure."

Major Sherwood read an ominous warning in their approach. He snapped at his orderly to close the tent flap, but the man was too slow. Pete Kitchen was already bulked solid in the tent opening. He threw his serape across his shoulder as he eyed the Major and said, "I have the honour of representing Jeb Logan according to the rules and regulations of dueling. As the challenged party you have the choice of weapons. Captain Slattery has consented to act as your second, Major Sherwood."

Sherwood got to his feet, backing away from the cold scrutiny of Pete Kitchen's eyes. "What . . . what sort of trumped-up drunken nonsense is this, anyhow?" he shrilled.

"Jeb Logan challenged you to a duel, openly on the streets of Tucson. Your answer was to have him whipped in public. Jeb Logan now demands satisfaction for his public humiliation."

"Jeb Logan," Sherwood appealed to the tall lawyer, "is a Quantrill outlaw, a renegade with a price on his head."

"Captain Jeb Logan," Slattery's cold, contemptuous voice cut in, "surrendered his sword to the Union Forces in Texas. There is no existing outlaw reward of any sort."

"Can't you see it's a dastardly plot to murder me, Thornton?" Sherwood gripped his attorney's arm. "This is the sort of thing Matt Durand warned you to guard against. It's premeditated murder!"

"Acting as your second," Captain Slattery cut in, "I named pistols as the choice of weapons. Colt pistols at a distance of twenty paces. Doctor Hand will be the surgeon in attendance." Slattery turned to Pete Kitchen and asked, "Is the hour of sunset suitable?"

"Sunset is agreeable. At the lightnin'-struck cottonwood in the clearing." Pete Kitchen's blunt thumb prodded Slattery's floating ribs. "Let's get the hell gone. Anything I can't stand is the sight of a man blubberin'."

"I will call here for you half an hour before sunset, Major Sherwood," Slattery informed him, clicked his boot heels and saluted.

"By God, this is high treason!" cried the Major. "I'll have you court-martialled, Slattery; drummed out of the army for this!"

But Captain Slattery and Pete Kitchen were already walking towards the ramada where Jeb Logan and Bob Leatherwood were waiting with Bill Ouray. They had overheard all that was said.

Pete Kitchen's grin was wide and satisfied as he slapped one of the wooden-handled Colt guns along Jeb's flank. "I've heard them Colt guns called 'widder makers'," he chuckled and slammed his hand down across Jeb's back. "By the hell, we got 'er made for you, Jeb Logan. Me'n Cap Slattery."

Jeb Logan forced a grin that left his eyes cold. He was wondering what sort of reaction Mona would have when she heard about the duel.

14

THE FUNERAL of Don Joaquín de la Guerra was as austere and forbidding as the man himself had been in the latter years of his life. No flowers, the token of sorrow and grief, banked the black coffin on the bare refectory table in front of the cold fireplace, where the old Spaniard lay in state below the portrait. Two faded, ragged old flags, the flag of Spain and the flag of the Republic of Mexico, draped the casket. The flags and the broken sword in the form of a cross held in skeleton hands paid military honour to the dead man.

The only music was the dismal chant that croaked from the throats of the paid mourners. The few tears shed by the Mexican women in the black shawls, who had come to mourn the dead, dried quickly, leaving no trace of sorrow. The women huddled together, trapped by the contagion of a vague fear that seeped into the yellowed adobe walls of the old casa. Their eyes cast furtive glances at the flickering candles in the tall silver candlesticks at either end of the coffin. None had the temerity to glance inside, lest the bitter old man's lidless staring eyes put a curse on them.

Much of the same tense dread held the men who stood together in small groups at the barn and corrals, as they drank from bottle and wine skin. All of them had the uneasy feeling that they trespassed here, which was, perhaps, the way the old Spaniard had anticipated it when he left a last request that the locked gate and barred door be thrown open to all.

Knowing all this, Padre Juan had held the rosary last evening and the Requiem Mass at dawn at the Mission San Xavier del Bac, leaving only the graveside services for today. He told Pedrito to toll the bell at the arched gate to summon those who had come.

The tolling of the bell sent a hush across the men, with a tendency to deaden the warmth of the liquor they had been consuming. They filed into the house with slow, reluctant step that quickened in cadence on the way out.

Padre Juan led the funeral procession to the little graveyard on a nearby knoll. The pine box with the remains of the old Pima, Coyote, was already there in its grave and the dirt shovelled in and rounded over. Not one of the Pimas was anywhere to be seen. They had buried their dead and vanished.

"God help that soldier who killed Coyote," Pete Kitchen read the meaning of their disappearance. He led the way from the graveyard after the burial. Jeb Logan walked beside him, the rest following behind.

Major Sherwood and the California lawyer, Thornton, and the squad of soldiers posted on guard around the tent, were the only men who had failed to attend the funeral. The late afternoon sun threw long shadows as the men walked slowly down the hill.

The funeral of Don Joaquín de la Guerra was over. There was nothing left here to stay the departure of those who had come. The priest was hastening their departure and when they had all left, he saddled the blue mule and rode away without a word or nod of farewell to any man.

"I reckon it's about that time, Cap," Pete Kitchen said to Slattery a little later. "Tell your man we'll be waiting for him at the lightin'-struck cottonwood. I'll fetch Doc Hand and Bob Leatherwood will furnish the likker in case the Major needs a brave-maker."

When Captain Slattery approached the army tent, Thornton, the attorney, stepped out to meet him. "Duelling is strictly forbidden in army rules and regulations, Slattery," he said. "This thing is contemplated murder!"

"Captain Jeb Logan, late of the Confederate Army, demands satisfaction for his public humiliation," said Slattery. "Major Sherwood violated both civil and army rules when he gave the order to tie Jeb Logan to the whipping post and have him lashed."

"What if Major Sherwood offers public apology?" the lawyer asked shrewdly.

"Public apology won't heal the scars on Logan's back, sir. If Major Sherwood is too cowardly to accept the challenge to a pistol duel, he is offered one, and only one, alternative."

"Name it," Thornton snapped.

"If Major Sherwood will submit to a lashing at the whipping post, Logan will withdraw his challenge and wield the lash." Captain Slattery turned his back on the lawyer and walked over to Jeb Logan standing with Pete Kitchen.

Thornton stood with clenched fists, his face livid with supressed fury. Then he turned and went into the tent. "You heard it, Sherwood," he said, anger and disgust in his voice. "Name your choice, and for God's sake, pull yourself together."

"Shut up, Thornton. You're paid to take orders, not to give advice."

Major Sherwood shoved past the lawyer and lurched out of the tent. His blue coat was open, the collar of his shirt unbuttoned, his mottled face slimed with cold sweat, knowing there was no outlet from the impending tragedy. Wiping the back of his hand across his mouth, the words blurted from loose lips. "I'll take the flogging!" Then he stiffened as he stared towards the arched gateway.

Jeb Logan and the others turned their heads in that direction. Sherwood's orderly was riding through, his horse spurred to a lope. He reined up in front of the Major and swung to the ground and whispered something to his officer. Whatever it was, it stiffened the Major's backbone. He wiped the sweat from his face with a handkerchief, and facing Jeb Logan he said, "My orderly reports that my wife has already left. It was on her account I refused to fight the duel. I gave her my promise I would not kill you, Logan. But circumstances have altered that. I was even willing to submit to a public horsewhipping rather than break my promise to Mona. Now, by God, I'm going to shoot you down!" Major Sherwood clinched the lie in a blustering voice as he faced his lawyer who was staring at him in open astonishment.

"I have no pistol, Thornton," Major Sherwood's voice was strident, arrogant. "You will make arrangements to borrow one of Logan's. By God, that will lend it an ironic touch. You will act as my second, Thornton, and make the proper arrangements. My orderly will accompany me to the duelling ground. Come inside, Sergeant, and close the tent."

"The cornered rat turned into a hellroarin' lion," said Pete Kitchen.

"There's a nigger in the woodpile," Bob Leatherwood said. "No coward turns bravo that quick."

Jeb Logan slid the pair of Colt guns from their holsters. Holding each gun by its barrel he held them out towards the attorney. "Take your choice," Jeb said. "Both guns have the same trigger pull and balance." His voice matched the bleakness of his eyes.

Thornton took one of the guns and walked away without a word.

"That lets me out," Captain Slattery said as he walked towards his troopers who were standing in the doorway of the barn. "Boots and saddles, Sergeant," he ordered quietly. "On the double. Fetch my mount when you report here at the stable."

"What's the rip, Captain?" the sergeant asked in a low voice.

"We're going after the nigger Bob Leatherwood mentioned. The one in the woodpile."

The lightning blasted old cottonwood tree was in the centre of a fifty yard clearing. Major Sherwood and Thornton, the lawyer, stood together on one side of the charred, bare-limbed tree. Jeb Logan and Pete Kitchen on the other side. Dr. Hand was at the base of the dead trunk, his shabby black leather bag on the ground.

Major Sherwood's staff sergeant stood with a four-man squad of soldiers at the edge of the brush. Bob Leatherwood and Bill Ouray stayed on the other side of the clearing.

The brush barrier screened the duelling ground. On either side of the Santa Cruz river and its wide valley the mountain peaks showed purple in the first twilight.

Jeb Logan's sharp scrutiny cut through the thin veneer of Sherwood's pompous arrogance and found the craven cowardice. Jeb had no pity for what he saw, but he had no stomach for the job ahead.

By arrangement with both seconds, Dr. Hand was to

act as official. The doctor was a big, powerful man, blunt to the point of brutality it was rumoured; outspoken in his strong likes and dislikes.

Dr. Hand motioned with both hands to Jeb Logan and Major Sherwood and said, "You two gentlemen will step over here. Stand back-to-back with your gun barrels pointed straight up so I can see them. I will count up to ten as you step off the required twenty paces. When you hear me call ten, you will turn and face one another, and fire at will. Is that understood?"

"Understood," Jeb Logan spoke first.

"Naturally," Major Sherwood blustered, his voice thin-edged.

Dr. Hand stepped back out of line of fire until his back was against the tree where Pete Kitchen and the lawyer were standing on either side.

The feel of the gun in Jeb's hand was a familiar thing that drove any qualms from his conscience. The memory of Fay Wayne and her golden hair flashed into his thoughts and left a cold hatred as he tilted his gun barrel skyward. If this be murder, then Jeb Logan would face it.

Major Sherwood stepped out at the start of the count. There was a set arrogant smile on his thick lips, and an almost fanatical gleam in his eyes as they flicked past his staff sergeant and beyond towards a brushy out-cropping of rimrock on a small pinnacle a hundred yards away. His step faltered at the count of eight. The sweat broke out, the stiff back slumped a little.

". . . Nine . . . Ten." Dr. Hand's voice fell heavily across the silence.

Jeb Logan whirled quickly. His thumb cocked the hammer as the gun came down. Major Sherwood's face looked ghastly now as he stood swaying, teetering unsteadily as if he were about to keel over. The cocked pistol in his hand was making vague, uncertain motions in Jeb's direction. Sherwood had the look of a man in some state of horrible catalepsy, brought on by stark, naked terror.

Jeb held his fire, staring at the man whose cowardice was so openly revealed. It was as if he was being forced to watch some revolting obscenity. Then the major's forefinger jerked spasmodically at the trigger as the gun barrel pointed aimlessly. The heavy recoil of the .44 Colt kicked

134

the gun from his loose grip and spun it through the air, the slug going harmlessly skyward.

Jeb heard Sherwood's shrill, terrified scream as he slumped face down, sobbing and slobbering his words. He stared at the man grovelling in the dirt, then picked up the gun and walked slowly back to where Pete Kitchen, the lawyer and Dr. Hand stood.

Captain Slattery rode into sight on the rimrock outcropping Major Sherwood had been watching. "Fetch the prisoner, Sergeant," he called back and rode down the steep, rocky brush-choked slant.

"Better attend to Sherwood, Thornton," Dr. Hand told the lawyer.

"To hell with him," Thornton said and walked away. "And to hell with this miserable farce," he added.

Jeb and Pete Kitchen walked over to Bob Leatherwood and Bill Ouray standing at the edge of the brush. The four men watched Major Sherwood lurch to his feet, looking around him fearfully, then walking towards the army ambulance that had brought him and the lawyer the quarter mile to the duelling ground.

Major Sherwood had almost reached his goal when Captain Slattery rode up to block the way, saluting stiffly as the Major looked up.

"I have a wounded soldier who needs to be taken in the ambulance to the army hospital at Camp Lowell, sir," Slattery said.

"To hell with him," Sherwood said gruffly.

"He is one of your own men. A Sergeant Burch. He's in critical condition. He was captured by Indians while he was hiding on the rimrock with a rifle, waiting to shoot Jeb Logan before the count of ten."

"A goddamned lie!" Sherwood shouted, hysterically.

"The Pimas slipped up on him from behind. They scalped him alive and left him there. They were paying off old Coyote's murder."

Major Sherwood's face was mottled, his eyes fearstricken as he lurched past the Captain's horse and crawled into the ambulance. "Get the hell under way!" he shouted at the soldier on the driver's seat.

"Hold it, soldier!" Captain Slattery barked. "You're taking Sergeant Burch to Camp Lowell as soon as Dr. Hand gives him first aid. That's an order, soldier!" Captain Slattery rode over to Jeb Logan and the other men. Trying to imitate Leatherwood's southern drawl, he said, "I done caught your nigger in the woodpile, Bob."

"That damn yankee son of a bitch was waiting to shoot Jeb Logan?" Leatherwood's question was waspish.

"That's what he told me. Said he was taking Major Sherwood's orders. Then he passed out."

"That's what religion does to Injuns," Pete Kitchen complained. "If them Pimas had been Apaches they'd a killed the gringo bastard."

As Slattery's cavalrymen came down the slope from the rimrock, supporting the wounded Burch straddle of his horse, the Captain rode over to where Sherwood's staff sergeant and squad of soldiers were standing around uneasily. Calling the orderly aside he said, "Let's have it, Sergeant."

"Have what, sir?"

"Major Sherwood sent you on horseback on an errand. You were gone an hour. You brought back a message. What the hell was the errand? I want the truth."

"Major Sherwood would bust me to a buck private if I spoke out of turn, sir."

"Major Sherwood is in no position to either harm you or do you any good. Come clean, or go back to Camp Lowell under arrest."

"The Major seldom drinks," the sergeant said, "but he was intoxicated when he told me to find Sergeant Burch and make him a proposition. He was to wait at an old adobe shack near here until he was sent for. When this pistol duel was forced on the Major, he sent me to tell Burch to go to the rimrock and before the count of ten he was to shoot to kill Jeb Logan. Sergeant Burch wears a sharpshooter's medal, sir. He was to be well rewarded for the job."

"As Major Sherwood's orderly, did you file a military dispatch from me on December twenty-second?" Slattery's cold eyes probed the man. "A dispatch sent by General Crook and signed by Captain Dennis Slattery, warning of a band of Apaches led by Chief Carnicero. Do you recall receiving that dispatch, Sergeant?"

"Yes, sir." The sergeant felt uncomfortable under the fixed stare.

"You'll be needed as a witness later, Sergeant, so keep your memory refreshed," Slattery told the soldier.

Captain Slattery's sunburnt face had a set, grim look as he reined off and dismounted beside the ambulance. The driver had taken the stretcher over to where Dr. Hand was examining the wounded Burch. The mules stood with slacked traces, the lines wrapped around the set brake. There was nobody within earshot when he mounted the rear step of the ambulance and went in.

Major Sherwood sat dejectedly at the far end, a half-emptied whisky bottle in his hand. He looked up with bleary eyes as Slattery dropped the canvas curtain behind him and sat down on a long bench.

"Get out!" Sherwood said belligerently. "Get the hell out of here or I'll prefer charges of insubordination!"

"You're in no shape to spring your rank on anybody, Sherwood," Captain Slattery said, taking his time about filling a short-stemmed, blackened briar pipe with tobacco and tamping it down with a blunt thumb.

"I once witnessed an army officer stripped of his rank," Slattery said, eyeing the major as he lit his pipe. "The luckless bastard had to stand at attention with his company in the early sunrise. The drummer stood to one side rolling his sticks on a snare-drum. And that was the only sound as the officer's brass buttons were torn from his uniform and the epaulets ripped from his shoulder straps. There was nothing left to show that he had ever been a soldier and a ranking officer of the United States Army. When his company marched off the parade ground, leaving the man alone, he was no longer a citizen of the United States. He was a man without a country. That night he blew out his brains."

Major Sherwood gripped the whisky bottle. The knuckles of his hand showed white as he lifted it and drank, swallowing the whisky like water. He lowered the bottle and looked at the hardbitten cavalry captain with pale, bloodshot eyes. "Horse manure!" he gritted.

Captain Slattery filled his lungs with tobacco smoke. He took a folded paper from his wallet and opened it, reading aloud:

"To the Commanding Officer at Camp Lowell, Tucson: From General Crook: Subject: You are hereby warned that a band of Apaches under the command of Chief Carnicero are on the war path. Carnicero is one of the most brutal savages known and I strongly advise that you provide all stage coaches to and from Tucson with sufficient military escort, and warn all passengers of the immediate danger."

Slattery eyed the other man coldly. "This dispatch was signed by me and sent by a messenger who risked his life travelling alone through Apache country. You were in charge that day, Sherwood, your commanding officer being absent. The message was read to you in the presence of the soldier I sent as a courier. It was ignored by you, filed and forgotten. No military escort was assigned to the stage coach, with its only passenger a woman who should not have been allowed to make the trip until the danger **was** over. She was a young and beautiful girl who had come to Tucson, misled by a false promise of marriage from you. I saw the pitiful remains of that jilted girl after the Apache Chief Carnicero left her."

Captain Slattery knocked the dead ashes from his pipe and continued talking. "You will be brought to trial for ignoring that military dispatch, Sherwood. And you'll be found guilty as hell." Slattery backed out of the ambulance, letting the curtain drop in place.

Major Sherwood's face was flushed from the whisky he had consumed as he just sat staring into space, making no move or uttering a word to defend himself.

Slattery picked up his bridle reins and led his horse. He beckoned to Sherwood's orderly. "Detail two men to carry Burch's stretcher to the ambulance. Burch is a military prisoner charged with murder. I hold you and Major Sherwood accountable for his safe arrival at Camp Lowell. Tell your soldiers to saddle up and ride armed escort. The ambulance will pick up the lawyer, Thornton. If he hesitates, tell him he's worn out his welcome at Hacienda del Jornada. Snap into it, soldier!" Slattery barked. He led his horse over to where Jeb Logan and Pete Kitchen and the others were.

There was a look in the cavalry officer's eyes that forbade questioning as the stretcher carriers loaded the unconscious soldier, and the ambulance got under way. "It's been quite a day," Slattery said to no one in particular. Then to Jeb Logan he said, "We'll be breaking up camp, Jeb. When Sergeant Burch comes up for trial, I'll need you for a witness."

Jeb gripped his outstretched hand. "Thanks for everything, Cap," he said warmly. "I'll be on hand when you need me."

15

"LA JORNADA!" Jeb Logan spoke aloud, liking the sound of the name as he sat his horse on a high peak that gave him a panoramic view that encompassed the entire vast holdings within the boundaries of a day's ride by the conquistador, Esteban de la Guerra. "La Jornada!" he repeated softly, almost reverently.

His was not the mere pride of possession as he viewed this empire of frontier wilderness that was his heritage, handed into his care and entrust by two men, his father and the blind Don Joaquín, last of the de la Guerra men. This vast empire of mountains and desert was a challenge to test the courage and fortitude and wisdom of any man.

The deep canyons and barrancas below were already purpled in the beginning of night, the barren rock cliffs of the highest peaks tinted crimson and gold as the shadows of twilight ended the day.

No man could look out and across this vastness without feeling the smallness of man and the almighty power of the Creator's hand in all its splendour and awesome beauty. Jeb was both proud and humble as he watched the shadows cover the last bright light on the furthermost peak like a candle flame snuffed out. Then he let his dun horse go down the steep slanting trail to Hacienda del Jornada.

It was moonrise when he approached the arched gateway and reined up. Standing in his stirrups he reached for the rawhide reata attached to the old Spanish bell that hung from the keystone of the arch above. The bong shattered the silence and at the third pull he let go the rope and pulled the wooden peg to open the pole gate, then rode through.

It had been almost a full month since the burial of Don Joaquín and Jeb had arranged the signal of the bell to announce his return. Pete Kitchen and Bob Leatherwood, who came over once a week from Tucson, were the two others who used the signal.

Hacienda del Jornada no longer had the forbidding look of neglect and desertion. A score of vaqueros and agrarian field labourers lived with their families in the many scattered adobe jacals that had been put in good repair. La Jornada assumed the look of a prosperous Mexican village on the banks of the Santa Cruz.

As Jeb approached, lights showed behind the heavy tapestry drapes pulled across barred windows of the whitewashed old casa. Blobs of light appeared in the scattered adobe jacals of the Mexican families. Late supper camp-fires spotted the clearing in the yards. Beyond a guitar strummed and a voice sang a plaintive love song.

"Don Jeb!" It was Pedrito who called out. He had just come from El Potrero Rancho, where Jeb had sent him for news of Pete Kitchen.

"How did you find Pete Kitchen?" Jeb asked.

"The patrón suffers. Tigers claw at his belly." Pedrito's eyes darkened with worry. "Doña Rosa sent you a large jar of wild honey."

"Consuela?" Jeb asked.

"She is at St. Joseph's Academy for Young Females in Tucson. The education is necessary, no?"

"Sí, *seguro*. Next you go to school at Tucson, eh Pedrito?"

"You have had an education, Don Jeb?" the boy asked.

"Public schools. Then military school in Virginia, a State in the Confederacy."

"El Capitán Slattery went to the school for soldiers?"

"West Point. Mostly Yankees from the north."

"The El Capitán is a true soldier. *Muy hombre!*" Pedrito said with admiration.

"I think it best for you to return to El Potrero, Pedrito. Your patrón is in poor health and you are needed there."

"*Gracias*, Don Jeb," Pedrito agreed readily.

A grey-haired Mexican in charge of the stables took Jeb's horse. He was one of Pedrito's uncles. His wife did the cooking at the main house.

141

Jeb found Bob Leatherwood eating a late supper. He grinned at Jeb, sizing him up from head to foot, liking what he saw.

"In less than a month you have fitted into this place like an old boot," Bob said lifting a glass of wine. "Don Jeb!" he saluted.

Once a week since Jeb Logan had taken possession of La Jornada, Bob Leatherwood had brought the mail from Tucson. Mostly it consisted of newspapers, but this time there was a letter. It was from Sherwood & Thornton, Attorneys, Fort Stockton, California. Bob indicated it with a nod, saying, "No doubt Matt Durand is contesting your claim to the La Jornada, Jeb. Wash up and sit down to as good a meal as ever went into an empty belly."

"Let's have the news, Bob, before you bust out at the seams."

"I'll fetch you up to date when you've had supper. News of any import, good or bad, is not conducive to good digestion," Leatherwood shoved back his chair from the table, evading Jeb's searching look.

"Quit stalling, Bob."

"Captain Dennis Slattery and his cavalry troop have been sent to Fort Yuma. Sherwood's Senator father pulled strings to have the Captain transferred, and any charges against Major Sherwood were squashed before they were born." Bob's voice was waspish when he added, "Major Sherwood is now commanding officer at Camp Lowell."

"Good God!" Jeb said, his hands clenched.

"Exactly," said Leatherwood. "He gave a champagne banquet for himself in honour of the event. His unkissed bride was conspicuous by her absence. She mysteriously dropped from sight the night she came back to Tucson from Don Joaquín's funeral with Solomon Warner and his wife. Durand's house remains vacant, the doors locked, the shutters closed. Sherwood lives alone in a house at Camp Lowell. It is my supposition that the marriage has never been consummated."

There was no warmth in Jeb Logan's eyes as they stared into the open fire, his back towards the speaker.

"Sergeant Burch," Leatherwood continued with the news, "anticipating his court-martial next week, crawled out the window of his room at Camp Lowell hospital.

His erstwhile pardner in crime, Tondro, was waiting outside with a horse and guns. They left without being halted or challenged."

Jeb swung around abruptly and asked. "When?"

"Sometime last night. The soldier on guard had apparently fallen asleep on post and it was sunrise before the alarm spread and Sherwood was located. The Major spent the night at California Mary's house of assignation." Leatherwood gestured with both hands. "That fetches the news up to the moment. Now wash up and get the wrinkles out of your belly, Jeb."

Jeb managed a grin as he left the room. "That tears it, Bob," he called over his shoulder. "Pete Kitchen bet Captain Slattery a beaver hat that neither Major Sherwood or Sergeant Burch would ever stand trial."

"Sure takes the rag offen the bush," Leatherwood replied.

Jeb pulled off his sweat-stained shirt and filled the wash bowl in his room. Making a quick toilet he returned to the supper table and ate in silence while Bob drank coffee and talked at random.

"Tondro and Matt Durand," Bob said, "had a big row and they've split up. Tondro has been blackmailin' Matt for years, bleedin' him white. When Tondro showed up after a long absence in Mexico he demanded that Matt deed the La Jornada lands over to him. Matt told him to go take a jump in the lake and had a gun in his hand at the time. Tondro was slicin' meat from a roast in Matt's kitchen when Matt backed him out the door with his hands up. That's how come Tondro's scalpin' knife was left there for Mona to pick up."

"Why didn't Durand kill Tondro then?"

"Because Sergeant Burch was outside the window. He called out for Matt to put up his gun or he'd gut shoot him. Then Tondro told Matt to think it over and if the land wasn't in his name in a week, he'd spill his guts. He had six scalps on his belt to back up his story; the story of how Matt Durand had hired him to kill off the six owners of the La Jornada land." Bob Leatherwood eyed Jeb across the table.

Jeb sat back in his chair, his eyes fixed on the flickering blaze in the huge fireplace. "What kind of a low-down human is Matt Durand?" Jeb asked, expecting no reply to his voiced thoughts. "Using his own daughter, quitting the country, leaving her married to a slimy . . . ?"

"The slimy bastard has a father who is a ruthless power when he greases his wheels with money and gets rolling, Jeb. A United States Senator from California. Matt Durand will come back to Tucson when the sign is right. By the way, did Pete Kitchen tell you that Matt told him he could name his price when he brought in Tondro's scalp?"

"Nope. Pete Kitchen knows how to talk a lot and say nothing," said Jeb.

"Pete has Tondro's scalpin' knife. He offered it to Durand to do his own scalpin'. It was after that Matt decided he needed some California air for the good of his health." Leatherwood quit his chair and walked over to where the latest copy of the Weekly Arizona Newspaper lay on the long table.

"It says here, Jeb," Bob read the item aloud: "Matt Durand is expected to return shortly from California, bringing with him Senator John Sherwood." Bob's voice was caustic. "The way I look at it," he said, "things are shaping up for a showdown. The law firm of Sherwood and Thornton are representing Matt Durand who has already sold the right-of-way through La Jornada to the railroad company, who had just completed a survey for a branch line into Mexico by way of Sonora. Matt got his own price and the lawyers handled the legal end, taking a big cut of the profits."

"Then the railroad will claim La Jornada?" Jeb asked grimly.

"Only the right-of-way, Jeb. But if the U.S. Government and the territory of Arizona recognize the claim of the deceased Wentworth Logan and you, as his heir, then Durand and the lawyers are in one hell of a shape and will be forced to pay you every dollar they made." Leatherwood sipped brandy before he took a big swallow and added, "Major Sherwood and Mona Durand are simply pawns in this game of dirty chess."

"You know what's happened to Mona, Bob? Where she is?"

"Safe and sound inside the cloistered walls of St. Joseph's Academy for Young Females. But keep it under

144

your hat. I gave Padre Juan my word I'd keep the secret."

Jeb picked up the letter from the lawyers and opened it casually, expecting to find some legal notice of contested claim. He grunted a little, like a man does when somebody pokes him unexpectedly in the belly.

"Mr. Jeb Logan," Jeb read aloud from the letter. "Dear Sir: It is urgently requested that you attend the meeting of the controversial land owners of the La Jornada Grant. The meeting will be held at 6 p.m. February 1st, at the Stage Station at Picacho Peak. Sincerely, Julius Thornton."

"It's a damn yankee trap," Leatherwood exclaimed acidly. "The stage station at Picacho Peak of all places! Why not Tucson? Don't be a sucker, Jeb."

"Sounds like a challenge," Jeb grinned flatly. "Tomorrow is the first of February. Six o'clock in the evening gives me plenty of time to make the ride."

"You're going?" Leatherwood asked with disbelief.

"I got it made," said Jeb. The cold glint in his eyes matched the flat-lipped grin. "Pedrito is leaving for El Potrero. I'll send word to Pete Kitchen." Jeb hesitated, thinking of a plausible reason for holding the meeting at Picacho Peak. "Could be it's a trick to get me away from here so they can move in and squat. Possession is nine-tenths of the law, Bob."

"I'll hold the fort, Jeb," Leatherwood rose to take the bait, hook, line and sinker. "Robert N. Leatherwood will see to it that no damn yankee carpetbagger moves in. I'll make a rebel stand, Jeb." He poured brandy into his cup as Jeb went out of the room, wiping a grin from his whiskered face. He was glad he wouldn't be dragging Bob Leatherwood in at the showdown. "Solong, Bob," he called across his shoulder as he went out to saddle up.

"Good huntin', Jeb. Watch behind you."

16

A ROUND white moon had come up after the brief winter twilight, prolonging the day as if holding its light for some tardy traveller bent on reaching a destination before dark.

The traveller could have been the white-maned padre, astride the stout blue mule, although the night held no fear for Padre Juan as he chewed on a mouthful of jerked meat and fingered the black beads. Neither rider nor mule was impatient or hurried, for theirs was a timeless mission. Sensing the priest's preoccupations, the mule sometimes stopped to grab a tuft of the curly grass and to take wise advantage of its patient rider. Content with the quiet stillness of the desert night, the priest rode on, unaware of the two men who watched from one of the many caves on the steep slope of Picacho Peak.

The bat caves along the rocky, steep slopes of the peak were the breeding and nesting places of the furry, winged animals, whose spread wings were fitted with needle sharp tiny barbs that clung to the rough surface as they slept by day. The guano was a foot thick dried mucous beneath the thin layer of fresh slime, foul-odoured and nauseous.

This was the hour of awakening for the night-prowling winged bats. They came awake with tiny, shrill rat noises that multiplied a hundred fold to pierce a man's eardrums like a surgeon's needle. The smaller man dodged as the first swarm of bats whirred past, black-winged, swift. He let out a thin scream, akin to terror.

The bigger man's ugly laugh taunted the other. "Scared of a flock of damned bats, you yellow-bellied soldier," Tondro sneered.

Tondro had lost sight of the mule and rider below, but he could see the lights of the stage station. It looked like

146

a lantern moving and he figured it would be the stock tender and that the stage had just rolled in. He looked down at the smaller man and asked, "You got the guts to go through with it, Burch?"

"I got the guts, Tondro," replied Sergeant Burch.

The two men headed down the steep, rocky slope for the brush thicket below. Tondro couldn't get his mind rid of the sight of the blue mule and its unknown rider, remembering the Negro he had killed who had been riding such a mule. He drained what was left in his bottle and tossed it back into the cave. It crashed with a muffled sound, scaring the rest of the bats out.

The high-cliffed peak threw a mile long black shadow across the desert below, with the pale winter moon behind it, as Jeb Logan rode towards the peak through the forest of giant saguaros. It was a ghostly, eerie place at night, this forest of cacti, and Jeb welcomed the tiny flicker of light beyond that told him he was nearing the stage station. He was almost at the end of the saguaro forest when he heard the distant, sharp crack of a rifle, then a spasmodic burst of shots that ended as suddenly as they had come, leaving an echo across the desert and then a silence pregnant with danger.

Jeb reined up and waited. He was keenly aware of the slightest movement of shadow against moonlight, the small sounds magnified as his every nerve became taut, the co-ordination of brain and muscle a hair-triggered reflex. It behoved a man to have his wits about him when split-second timing was a thin, fragile barrier between life and death.

Jeb rode on and as he came into gun range he saw the lighted lantern that hung on a low branch of the big old mesquite tree in front of the adobe stable and adjoining corral. Within the radius of its light was the empty stage coach. The six-horse team had been unhooked, unharnessed, watered and fed grain and hay in the feed yard. The fresh team, harnessed beforehand, waited inside the barn, each team in its stall.

Just within the lantern light was the army ambulance, its canvas curtain down, the mule team still wearing harness in a double stall inside the barn.

There was no sign of the stage or ambulance drivers,

nor was there any visible sign of the stock tender and barn man, who should be busy greasing the wheels of the coach that had arrived not too long ago and helping the stage driver fit horse collars and pads, checking straps and buckles. Jeb knew that something was wrong in the absence of the usual bustle.

Lamplight showed through the windows and open doorway of the low thatch-roofed adobe house where the stage coach passengers and driver ate a hasty meal, while the teams were being changed. The homemade plank door of the eating house gaped open in spite of the winter chill in the night air, the heavy door held back by the booted feet and legs of a man who lay motionless across the threshold.

The man was dressed in a well-tailored suit of black broadcloth, a clawhammer coat and pants fitted with boot-straps. There was a high polish to the black boots. His head lay sideways to profile the face with its carefully trimmed mutton-chop side whiskers and heavy moustache that were the iron-grey colour of his thick mane that touched the edge of his starched white collar. A handsome, stalwart man with waxen face and pale eyes glazing in death. A pool of blood was slowly creeping across the wide plank step from the gaping bullet wound that had torn through vest and starched white shirt and lower ribs.

The tall man who stood straddle of the dead body had to lower himself to a half crouch to peer in through the open door, the long-barrelled Colt pistol in his hand swinging in a flat arc. "Don't nobody move," the man said, his voice saw-edged. "You seen what happened to that high and mighty son of a bitch who tried to leave." He backed away from the door and into the shadow.

Jeb Logan had left his horse behind some brush and from where he crouched low alongside the mesquite corral he could see into the room that was both a saloon and eating place. The bar was used to stack filled and empty dishes to be taken into the lean-to kitchen that had a short swinging half-door. A strip of wagon canvas served as a table cloth on the large round poker table. A rotating stand in the centre of the table held the salt and pepper and sugar bowl. Half a dozen tin plates and cups were placed around the table and a divided box held the knives, forks and spoons. Bowls and platters piled with food were

148

on the table along with a blackened coffee pot. Bar room chairs had been hastily shoved back and three men, whose supper had been abruptly interrupted, stood backed against the wall, arms raised, the fourth lay dead across the threshold.

Big, paunchy Matt Durand stood with his legs braced, hands lifted to the level of his shoulders. His red face was congested, almost purple with helpless fury. A soggy half-smoked cigar was clamped in the corner of his wide mouth.

Major Sherwood stood next to him, his face the colour of putty, his arms raised high, the wall bracing his sagging back. Thornton, the lawyer, leaned against the wall, tall, cold eyed, poker faced, somehow managing to retain something of his judicial manner with his arms lifted.

The man outside moved back into the doorway, straddling the dead man with long legs, and Jeb Logan got his first good look at Tondro, a big rawboned man in moccasins and buckskin shirt and tight pants that had long ago lost colour beneath the layers of grease and dried blood and dirt. A wide belt, loops bristling with cartridges, sagged crosswise around his lean belly, the holster empty, the long-barrelled gun in his hand. The hilt of a Bowie knife showed in a hard rawhide Indian scabbard looped to the belt. Tondro's straight black hair came below his shoulders in greasy twisted locks. A tangled, matted beard grew along his long pointed, underslung jaw, and a drooping moustache came down across the corners of his mouth. A thin, high-beaked nose hooked down to his upper lip. The bloodshot yellow eyes took on a pale greenish glow, like the eyes of a cougar.

"You got that deed to La Jornada on you, Thornton?" Tondro asked in a rasping voice. "Everybody signed up?"

"It's in my brief case there on the bar, signed by Matt Durand, Senator Sherwood and his son, and myself."

"How about Mona Durand, Thornton? It needs her John Hancock."

"I have her power of attorney. I signed in her behalf," Thornton told him.

"I'll take it up with the high-toned lady," Tondro grinned obscenely, "when I get around to it some moonlit evenin'."

"You go anywhere near Mona," Matt Durand clenched

his big hands that were on the level with his shoulders, "and you'll wish you'd been born dead, you dirty black-mailin' bastard!"

Tondro's laugh was short, ugly. "You seen what happened to this big politico dawg when he got outa line. He's one hell of a big Senator now, ain't he? Just one more carcass for the maggots." The gun in Tondro's hand made a flat arc as his teeth bared in a twisted grin to show his broken teeth.

"Let's have that deed to La Jornada, lawsharp," Tondro said.

Thornton lowered his hands and unbuckled the straps of the leather brief case and took out a long brown manila envelope. "I notified Jeb Logan and Pete Kitchen of this meeting. They should be showing up anytime now," Thornton said.

"The hell you say!" Tondro grabbed the envelope and with a lithe swiftness, he moved to one side of the door and into the dark shadow outside the adobe house. Crouched there his long arm snaked out and dragged the dead Senator Sherwood clear. Then he lifted a big foot and slammed the door shut, reaching around the corner to fasten it by a hasp lock on the outside.

Jeb Logan's trigger finger had been itching for a long while as he held a gun in each hand, but he had held his gunfire, stayed by an intense curiosity to see what Thornton's game was.

It appeared to Jeb that the shrewd lawyer had planned it for Jeb and Pete Kitchen to shoot it out with Tondro, knowing this would happen if the men met face to face. But somehow Tondro had gotten control and it seemed as if the California lawyer was too crafty to have let it happen unless he had planned it that way. That deed was of no value. Tondro was little better than a moron. He couldn't read or write. A gun and scalping knife and the cowardly cunning to use the lethal weapons were all that the il-literate giant possessed.

Jeb saw the light inside the house suddenly go out. The three men inside were armed. Tondro should have killed them while he had the chance instead of letting them stay alive, Jeb thought.

Jeb could make out the dim outline of Tondro as he

moved in the black shadow of the wall. "Burch!" Tondro's saw-edged voice lifted. "Where the hell you gone?"

"I'm on guard out back, like you said to be," Burch answered in a whisky thick voice.

"That shyster said Jeb Logan and Pete Kitchen were due to show up," Tondro said.

"Then it's time we got the hell gone, Tondro."

"Both doors are locked from the outside," Tondro said, ignoring Burch's idea of leaving. "Get that can of coal oil from the woodshed and throw some on the back door and the roof and set fire to it. Then fetch the can around front. They'll have to come out the window, one at a time."

"You figger on shootin' 'em as they come out, Tondro?"

"Hell, yes, and scalp 'em to boot. I told you we'd make it look like the Apaches were here and gone. Swill some rotgut for a brave-maker and set that fire, while I lift the Senator's scalp. We'd better work fast before Jeb Logan and Pete Kitchen get here."

Jeb broke out in a cold sweat. He'd held back too long. All he could do was to sit tight until Tondro came back to the front door.

Jeb saw the flicker of fire as the first flames licked the back of the house. Then he caught sight of Burch as he came around the corner, his head wrapped in a soiled, dirty white bandage. As he passed the dark window a gun spewed fire from within. Burch let out a howl of pain as the lead slug struck his shoulder, knocking him sideways. He dropped the can of coal oil and grabbed at the window sill. Clinging with his free hand, he shoved his gun at the window and commenced shooting, his drunken voice cursing.

Somewhere a mule's raucous braying filled the night. Jeb's dun horse behind the corral nickered a shrill answer. Then Jeb saw the blue mule, terrified by the crackling fire, round the corner on a run, ears laid back, tufted tail in the air. Jeb saw Tondro as he sprang up from his crouch, then go down as the mule rode over him. He let out a hoarse animal sound of stark nameless fear.

Jeb straightened up from his crouch and yelled at Tondro, who had scrambled to his feet and started running, but Jeb's voice was drowned out by Burch's howling and the gunfire.

Jeb ran after Tondro. His loping gait had a lurch and Jeb knew the shod mule hoofs had done damage. Tondro had a gun in one hand, a knife in the other. He made a sinister, grotesque figure with his long black hair wild. His whiskered face was a bloody mask from the mule's hoofs and blood was smearing the dirt glazed buckskin shirt.

Jeb angled to cut Tondro off. "TONDRO!" he shouted wildly as he ran. This time Tondro heard and twisted his head around. Tondro tripped, lost his balance and fell. He was up on one knee when he saw Jeb Logan a couple of hundred feet away. Tondro fired wildly and Jeb felt the heavy slug as it plowed a furrow along his thigh, knocking him off balance.

Jeb fired both guns as he went down. Tondro let out a scream and fell sideways, his greasy hair falling across his dead face. Around his hat that had fallen off was a band of black human hair, similar to the one Bob Leatherwood had picked up in Madera Canyon.

Jeb saw the red flames licking up into the sky from the lean-to kitchen. He lurched like a drunken man as he tried to break into a run on his wounded leg and fell flat.

In the angry glow of the fire Jeb saw Major Sherwood come out through the window of the main room in a headlong plunge. The cocked gun in his hand exploded as it pointed downward at Sergeant Burch crouched below. The bullet struck the soldier's face under the bandaged head with a terrific force that tore his jaws apart, ending his blasphemy, jerking his trigger finger to send a bullet into Sherwood's chest. The dead major hung across the sill, his bulk filling the small window.

Jeb got to his feet and with a painful, crabwise gait he ran towards the burning building. He hammered the locked hasp free with his gun barrel, and swung the door open. A billowing wave of black-grey smoke enveloped him. He went down on all fours, then pulled his loosely knotted neck handkerchief up across his mouth and nose for protection. Smoke filled his eyes, blinding him a little, as he crawled through the door and across the pine board floor. He found Matt Durand overcome by smoke, his shirt wet with blood, and dragged him outside. A shower of sparks geysered over them as the burning roof collapsed.

Jeb waited until the shower of sparks quit falling, then he dragged Major Sherwood from where he hung in the window. He laid the dead major alongside his dead father.

Jeb was squatted beside Matt Durand, searching for some sign of life when the big man groaned and opened his eyes. "Was it you, Jeb Logan, that killed Tondro?" he asked.

"Yes." ,

"Tondro killed your father. But he was just a hired hand. A wolfer collecting bounties on white men's scalps. It was Senator Sherwood and Thornton's money paid for everything. That pair of white-collared dudes stayed in California and never got within smelling distance of the men they paid Tondro to murder. They sent the money to me and I had to pay Tondro his blood money. But I want you to know, Logan, I never hired Tondro to kill your father or any of the La Jornada land holders."

"Why did you sit back all these years and take the blame?"

"I'd gambled away a lot of money belonging to the Butterfield Overland Stage Line, and their attorneys, Sherwood & Thornton, made my loss good out of their private bank accounts, making me sign a confession, which they have held over my head like a double-bitted axe for fifteen years. I was their go-between, the middle man for all their dirty chores."

The stocky Pete Kitchen, his serape over one shoulder, a carbine cradled in one arm, stepped around the corner of the burning house. The carbine was pointed with contemptuous carelessness at the California lawyer, Thornton, who walked with dragging, reluctant step about fifty feet ahead of Pete, hands lifted to the level of his shoulders. The lawyer's clothes were dirty, the white collar and tie ripped off, his face drained of blood.

"This law-sharp dragged Padre Juan off his mule, pistol whipped him and stole the mule. The mule spooked at the sight of the fire and threw him just as I rode up and caught him before he got away. He offered me a thousand

153

dollars for the loan of my horse, but I put the padre on the horse and used a little persuasion to bring this feller in on foot."

Matt Durand had propped himself up on his left elbow. His right hand reached out quickly and pulled Jeb's gun from its holster. "Fill your hands, Thornton!" Durand barked as Jeb stepped quickly to one side.

Thornton had his gun pulled when Matt shot him in the breast bone. The lawyer was dead before he slumped to the ground.

"I'm obliged, Logan," Matt said, and handed the gun to Jeb, "for the loan of your gun."

"How did Thornton get out of the fire alive?" Jeb asked, as Pete Kitchen held a bottle of whisky he'd taken from his hip pocket to Matt's lips and let him swallow a couple of times.

"Bought his way out before Burch set the fire. He called to Burch on guard out back and bribed him with money and the promise to clear him of the murder charge and army desertion. Burch let him out and barred the back door on us. Then that bastard son-in-law of mine shot me just before he tried to climb out the window," Matt explained.

Durand's bloodshot, pain-squinted eyes looked into Jeb's. He said, "Looks like I'm cashing in my chips. I could die with a free mind if you'd promise to take care of my girl, Jeb. Mona fell in love with you but I was forced into making her marry Sherwood. I've dealt you a lot of hell, Jeb, but if it isn't too much to ask I'd like to know you'll look out for Mona."

Jeb grinned faintly. "It's the easiest promise a man ever made. It'll be up to Mona. She's a widow now. Burch killed Major Sherwood as he went out the window."

"All you need, Jeb, is Mona to go with La Jornada. She's got a sort of right to live there, at that, on her mother's side. I married Ramona de la Guerra."

Padre Juan rode up and dismounted. He bent over the wounded man.

"If you can patch me up to stand the trip to Tucson, Padre," Matt Durand said, "I'll die happy. I want to live long enough to see my daughter before I go on the long ride."

Tondro and Burch had run off the stock tender and his wife and the stage driver. Now they were all back. The woman was back in the kitchen and the two men were hooking the six-horse team to the stage coach. Cushions and lap-robes were made into a bed for Durand. Padre Juan said he would ride inside the stage with him.

The bullet rip in Jeb's thigh was a minor wound and he was able to ride with Pete Kitchen. The soldier who had driven the ambulance for Major Sherwood to Picacho Peak had been killed by Burch. Now the stock tender would drive it back, loaded with the dead.

Matt Durand was being carried gently into the stage coach when the lonesome wail of a locomotive whistle echoed dismally in the night. Matt lifted his head to listen, a strange smile twisting his mouth. In a weakening voice he said, "The railroad has come at last. The price they agreed to pay for the right-of-way through La Jornada to Sonora, Mexico, will now be paid to Jeb Logan when the railroad picks up their option. This will be the last stage to run across Arizona Territory. I rode the first one across. Now I'm taking the last one."

When the stage got underway Jeb Logan and Pete Kitchen rode behind it in silence for a long time. Then Pete said, "Maybe Matt will be alive when we get to Tucson, but most likely he'll be dead when the stage pulls in for the last time."

"How do you feel, Pete?" Jeb inquired. "Pedrito said you were having more trouble."

"Guess I'll have to have my gizzard cut out, and stop eating chili beans. A helluva note for a man," Pete said, then added, "But I'll put off the operation until Pedrito and Consuela are married."

"They'll both be away in school for a few years before they can marry, Pete, so you better have the operation right away. I'll look after your ranch while you're gone," Jeb promised.

"Then I guess I'll let the Doc cut me up. The sooner the better, he told me."

"I dug up the twenty-five thousand in gold Don Joaquín buried under the wine barre. One half will go to Padre

Juan for his mission work. The rest will go to educate Pedrito and Consuela. When they marry, I want them to live at La Jornada for the rest of their lives."

"You're a good man, Jeb Logan," Pete said, meaning it.

17

IT WAS no hallowed ground, this bare six foot strip of land, packed hard by countless bare and sandalled feet and circled by rings of thickly-packed earth a foot high. A youthful sinner, some say an adulterer, met a violent death on this spot and his body was buried within the earth circle. It is said that the young woman, the cause of the sin and the murder, crept back to the unmarked grave under the cover of night, to burn the first candle there, kneeling, black-shawled, to pray. If the candle should burn through the night, then the murdered youth's soul would be freed. Daylight had found the tiny flame still flickering, so the woman arose and went away, to return no more, the wishful prayer answered.

It seemed to Jeb Logan that all the candles ever made were burning there now, placed close together to fill the earthen circle, some in lamp chimneys or broken bottles set in old layers of candle grease that carpeted the ground below the crumbling adobe wall of the Wishing Shrine in El Barrio Libre, the Free District of the Old Pueblo of Tucson. This was the poor section of town. The adobe jacals, the tin roof supported by saguaro-ribbed walls, seemed to huddle together as the occupants shared their misery.

Human derelicts came here to die without hope, living within the broken crust of lost dreams, sodden with the stupor of forgetfulness that comes from drinking mescal. El Barrio Libre, the graveyard of the living dead.

Lighting their candles, keeping the night's vigil, the feeble candle flames seen through the vacant, bleared eyes of the outcasts, the Wishing Shrine a last earthly refuge of forlorn hope.

Jeb Logan had wandered here alone in the dark hour

before the false dawn, not knowing where he was going, nor caring; not knowing where he was when he stopped at the pool of candlelight. An old Mexican, barefoot and in rags, lay on his back near the adobe wall, an empty bottle in his hand. An old woman, a rusty black *rebozo* over her thin white hair, gummed toothless words as she watched a tiny flame inside a broken, blackened lamp chimney. Near her a young girl with bare legs, her faded cotton dress tight over a pregnant belly, warm brown eyes dark shadowed with memories of broken promises of eternal love, watched the flame of a candle in a bottle. Somewhere beyond in the jacals of El Barrio Libre a guitar sounded in minor chord, where a few Mexicans shared a bottle and song.

Jeb was unaware that he was being followed until the hushed voice said behind him, "I came early, Don Jeb." It was Pedrito who spoke. "I came to light two candles I purchased at Don Solomon's store, and to make two wishes, one for you and one for me. I used nothing to shelter the flame from the wind, and it is still burning." He pointed to the smoked, broken lamp chimney and the old woman, and said, "The old one is without hope; therefore she cheats."

Jeb and Pedrito sat on the ground, their backs against the adobe wall. There was no need of words and they remained silent in their own thoughts. Matt Durand had died during the night. Mona and Padre Juan were with him. Jeb had seen Mona when he and Pete Kitchen had ridden up in the dust behind the stagecoach. Their eyes had met, but Mona had looked at him without recognition, her face pale, her lips pulled together in a thin line.

Jeb had washed up at Bob Leatherwood's house and put on a new suit of clothes, boots and a Philadelphia hat that Bob had brought for him from Solomon Warner's store. He had a drink from Leatherwood's bottle and had wandered off alone with his brooding thoughts, until his aimless wanderings had led him to the Wishing Shrine.

Jeb closed his heavy-lidded eyes now and was only half awake some time later when Pedrito gripped his arm, excitement in the boy's whispered words.

"Madre de Dios!" Pedrito crossed himself with swift, furtive motion. "Behold the two wishes I made come true.

158

It is Consuela and Mona Durand." Pedrito was on his feet, pulling at Jeb's jacket. The boy hurried to greet Consuela, taking her by the hand and walking away.

Mona was dressed in black and as she walked alone, Jeb went out to meet her. There was no need of words between them as he took her into his arms.

Walt Coburn was born in White Sulphur Springs, Montana Territory. He was once called "King of the Pulps" by Fred Gipson and promoted by Fiction House as "The Cowboy Author". He was the son of cattleman Robert Coburn, then owner of the Circle C ranch on Beaver Creek within sight of the Little Rockies. Coburn's family eventually moved to San Diego while still operating the Circle C. Robert Coburn used to commute between Montana and California by train and he would take his youngest son with him. When Coburn got drunk one night, he had an argument with his father that led to his leaving the family. In the course of his wanderings he entered Mexico and for a brief period actually became an enlisted man in the so-called "Gringo Battalion" of Pancho Villa's army.

Following his enlistment in the U.S. Army during the Great War, Coburn began writing Western short stories. For a year and a half he wrote and wrote before selling his first story to Bob Davis, editor of *Argosy-All Story*. Coburn married and moved to Tucson because his wife suffered from a respiratory condition. In a little adobe hut behind the main house Coburn practiced his art and for almost four decades he wrote approximately 600,000 words a year. Coburn's early fiction from his Golden Age—1924–1940—is his best, including his novels, *Mavericks* (1929) and *Barb Wire* (1931), as well as many short novels published only in magazines that now are being collected for the first time. In his Western stories, as Charles M. Russell and Eugene Manlove Rhodes, two men Coburn had known and admired in life, he captured the cow country and recreated it just as it was already passing from sight.

ß